MURDER AT THE PUB

A gripping cozy crime mystery full of twists

JANE ADAMS

A Rina Martin Mystery Book 6

Originally published as
Cause of Death

Revised edition 2022
Joffe Books, London
www.joffebooks.com

First world edition published by Severn House Publishers
Ltd in Great Britain and the USA in 2012

Trade paperback edition first published by Severn House
Publishers Ltd in Great Britain and the USA in 2012

Cover art by Dee Dee Book Covers

ISBN: 978-1-80405-073-6

PROLOGUE

They had driven from the harbour up through the little village and out into open country. It was likely no one had seen them, though a few curtains may have twitched at the sound of cars passing through so late. Those who lived here were farm workers and fishermen. At this time of year they rose early and fell into bed when the sun went down; slept the sound sleep of the justifiably exhausted.

Despite the late hour it was still surprisingly light, a gibbous moon and more stars than Jerry could ever recall seeing before lending a surprising amount of brightness to the proceedings. He took time to admire the silvered light on the fields and, as the road briefly swung back on itself, the sheen on the sea. They were early; he could see the line of trees that marked their destination. Jerry did not want to be the first to arrive.

He was driving the lead car, Santos beside him in the front seat, designated spokesman as his French was better than Jerry's. In the 4x4 behind them were two of the newbies: Skelton and Hughes. Jerry thought Skelton was a good man, but he was far from certain about Hughes, and far from happy that the boss should pick such an important and potentially difficult moment to test them out.

'There,' Santos said, indicating a turn just as Jerry spotted it. He swung on to the track between the trees and into the woodland, pulling up a few hundred yards along the track and, out of a habit of caution, easing the car round in a multi-point turn so they were heading in the right direction for a fast exit. Santos glanced across but said nothing, while Skelton, driving the second vehicle, took his lead from Jerry and did the same—in considerably more moves, Jerry was amused to note. A snort from Santos told him his companion had shared his observation.

They got out. Jerry slipped the keys into one of the many pockets of the photographer's vest he habitually wore, but did not bother to lock the doors. Santos carried the pilot case and the four of them moved off down the track, pine needles soft beneath their feet, the scent of damp earth and resinous trees filling Jerry's nostrils.

'Lights,' Santos muttered.

Jerry nodded. He'd already seen them. Fifty yards on and the track opened out into one of the many fire breaks that crisscrossed this forestry land. Two men stood in the centre of the clearing and Jerry spotted at least three more standing in the shadow of the trees. Their contacts had brought their vehicles right into the clearing, headlamps on. They stood, silhouetted against the light, and Jerry edged sideways, aiming to get a better view. Behind him he felt Skelton do the same.

Santos moved forward and lowered the pilot case to the ground. His opposite number came forward, knelt down and crouched over an armoured box, releasing the catches with a sharp sound that was overloud in such a quiet place. So far, so good, Jerry thought, but the feeling that something wasn't right had been growing upon him as they entered the clearing and it wouldn't go away.

And then all hell broke loose. Voices shouting from the tree line. Lights. A man yelling '*Attendez!*'—and then the gunfire.

Jerry hit the deck a split second after Santos. Hughes was down, shot and unmoving. Skelton was wounded too; Jerry could hear him swearing as he struggled to get under cover.

'Get the hell out of here,' Santos hissed. He rolled and ran, keeping low, and Jerry wriggled to where Skelton writhed and moaned. He grabbed him and dragged; Skelton tried to help by half kicking, half crawling, and somehow they made it back into the cover of the trees.

'Got to get to the cars,' Jerry said. 'Can you make it?'

'I don't know. What the fuck is going on?' He was gasping for breath.

'Where are you hit? Shit!' He dragged Skelton deeper under the trees, wishing they had more cover. The regimentation of the forestry planting offered little defence if one of the powerful lights shone their way. Behind them in the clearing the shooting continued, and Jerry blessed the fact that those they had come to meet were more numerous and better armed than his group had been, though to get into a shoot-out with what he assumed must be the authorities seemed like madness. The place would become a killing ground.

Right now, though, he was not about to question good fortune. He fumbled in a pocket of his jacket for the med pack, found a bandage, wrapped it tight around Skelton's thigh. His photographer's vest was a bit of a joke with the others. They called it his utility belt, and the fact that he often had the camera to go with it and actually did take pictures caused additional hilarity. Just now, though, Jerry thought Skelton would not be seeing the funny side.

'All right, let's go.'

He hauled Skelton to his feet, taking most of his weight as he wrapped the man's arm around his shoulders. Together they staggered forward. Jerry was listening, hoping. The last thing he wanted was for the shooting to stop and armed police to move out again into the trees. The other fear was that they'd reach the cars and find others waiting for them. Ears straining, Jerry heard an engine fire up and something drive away.

'Santos,' he said. He hoped. So long as they could reach the 4x4 then they had a chance.

Knowing time was against them and feeling Skelton's weight increase with every step, he decided to take a risk. He turned sharply, leading them back on to the track. He paused, shuffling Skelton's body into a better position. 'We've got to move fast, right?'

There was no response. Skelton's feet dragged. Jerry could feel him trying to take steps, but his injured leg was limp now and most of the forward momentum was down to Jerry.

Behind them the gunfire died down and voices reached them across the sudden void of silence. Jerry swore. He dragged Skelton faster, harder. Skelton moaned. Fifty yards more. Somehow they made it and Jerry shoved the injured man into the back seat, thankful for the caution that had led him to leave the vehicle facing the right way.

He started the engine, suddenly aware of movement on the path behind, and also of a shadow detaching itself from the forest and running across the track ahead.

'Fuck.' Jerry gunned the engine and released the handbrake, surging forward. Someone behind them fired a shot. It went wide but shattered glass in the offside wing mirror. The figure up ahead raised a weapon. Jerry accelerated and the figure dived out of the way. Then they were out on to the road.

Jerry drove, not sure what direction to take or if he should be heading back towards the coast. He drove for an hour before taking the risk of stopping, and only then did he pause long enough to take a look at Skelton. The man lay very still, half on half off the back seat, and Jerry confirmed what he had already guessed. Skelton hadn't made it.

He travelled on, making guesses at each junction until he reached a main road. He stashed the car and body in a farmer's field and then, taking his backpack and camera, hitched a lift back to the coast and caught a ferry home.

The journey gave him time to think, and the more he thought about it the more wrong it all felt. Nothing on the news, nothing in the papers on either side of the Channel. Only the ongoing scandals that had hit the media a few weeks before: government departments implicated in the illegal sale of arms and intelligence; three high-level politicians and some very senior civil servants handing in their resignations.

Santos met him off the ferry. He'd made it back a day ahead.

'Two men down. Boss isn't best pleased,' Santos said.

'No, I can imagine losing that amount of cash isn't going to go down well.'

Santos laughed. 'What happened to Skelton?'

Jerry told him, briefly. Santos shook his head. 'Should have put a bullet in his head and left him in the woods,' he said. 'Wasted your time, didn't you? Boss wouldn't look kindly on you if you'd got yourself arrested. He's mad as hell, wants to know who sold us out.'

They weren't police, Jerry thought, but something stopped him saying it out loud.

ONE

He watched the men come out of the pub. Three he knew: Jerry Mason, Santos, whose last name seemed to change with his mood, and Tomas James. Woe betide anyone who tried to insert an h into his name.

The other two were not familiar, and from the way the group moved it was obvious that they were new to Santos and the rest. To his practised eye there was a definite division, not a sense of hostility, but simply of the familiar versus the not yet tested. He knew the form because he would have behaved in exactly the same way towards newcomers—and had been on the receiving end of such treatment too.

Stan Holden was suddenly possessed by an odd desire to go over and talk to them, not to provoke a confrontation exactly—he was good, but he knew when he was well out-numbered—but just to get a response. They'd know he was out; it was something their boss would have been sure to keep a note of. He'd been Stan's old boss and the relationship had not ended on a good note, but Stan Holden felt oddly san-guine about that. Yes, the threat was there, but if Haines had wanted him dead then an accident could have been arranged while Stan was still inside. No, for the moment he wasn't registering sufficiently high on the radar for his life, death or unfortunate accident to be of top concern. Presently, to attack Stan would mean drawing unwanted attention, and he knew instinctively that, though his time might come—Haines not being the kind of man to even *understand* the concept of bygones being bygones—it was not yet.

He watched the five men as they moved away. This was the clearest indicator yet that his old governor had moved back and was operating again in this neck of the woods. He'd heard rumours this past year, but not been sure if they were just phantoms and legends or had some root in actual fact. Now he knew.

Stan drew back into deeper shadow. Santos was jumpy, glancing round, eyes everywhere, but it was Tomas that concerned him more. The man barely seemed to register his environment most of the time, but Stan knew he missed nothing. He had an almost uncanny instinct for trouble, and Stan had no wish to draw attention to himself—odd impulses towards bravado excepted. Tomas was dangerous in unpredictable ways, unlike Santos and Jerry Mason who were both eminently predictable, paid muscle—much like Stan had been when in the same line of work. But Tomas was something else again. Subtle as a knife, Coran had once said, and the more Stan thought about it, the more he agreed with Coran, a man now dead, gone and ungrieved. Subtle as a stiletto, Stan thought. That didn't sound quite as good but it was far more apt. Sharp and pointed and slim enough not to be noticed until it was wedged between your ribs and killing you.

He wondered briefly about the other two, observing them carefully as they stepped out under a street light, one pausing to light a cigarette before moving on. Stan took note of the dark hair, the slight but muscular build and the designer stubble on the chin. *That* drew his particular attention. So, Haines was not close by; they had been sent out either on a few days' R & R or they were preparing for something before the big man arrived. Haines was a stickler for personal appearance and would not have tolerated one of his men going unshaved.

Interesting, Stan thought. He pulled back again as Santos glanced around, and this time Tomas turned as well, pausing and staring towards the pub they had just left.

Time to go, Stan thought, backing off slowly and then slipping away down the alley at the side of the inn and back over the wall into the office car park beyond. He was happier once he'd reached the relative anonymity of the main road and the scant crowds now also leaving pubs and restaurants as the church clock struck the hour. Eleven. Stan counted automatically, though he was fully aware of what time it was.

So, what now?

Nothing, yet. Time to wait and see. Good job he'd always been the patient type.

TWO

Rina Martin stood in the hall of Peverill Lodge and studied her mail: bill, junk, a letter for Tim from someone whose writing she didn't recognize, and a card saying she had missed a parcel. It was this last she was finding aggravating. Not only had she not been expecting a parcel, but she had only been in the kitchen when the post had come tumbling on to the mat, and if there had been something too big for her letterbox, then why on earth had the postman not rung the bell? Had she been quicker getting to it, then she would have opened the door and accosted the cause of her annoyance and demanded an explanation. As it was, she'd been too busy minding the bacon and eggs and by the time she had come through to collect the letters, the recalcitrant man was long gone, his red bag and blue uniform now just visible at the other end of Newell Street. The not so nice end.

Irritated, she set the letters on the side table next to the phone and went back to the kitchen to put the kettle on the hob. There were sounds coming from upstairs that told her the family was awake and slowly descending. From the thump directly above her, Tim had more or less fallen out of bed. He'd been very late home last night, Rina thought, and wondered how the new show at the Palisades had gone.

First down the stairs and floating into the kitchen were the Peters sisters, Bethany and Eliza, still in their pyjamas and pink satin gowns with their grey, bobbed hair tied up with chiffon bows. They kissed Rina good morning before settling on one side of the big, scrubbed table. Breakfast at Peverill Lodge was always eaten in the kitchen, the occupants only moving to the dining room for lunch, tea and dinner. It was also the only meal that Rina regularly cooked. The Montmorency twins, Matthew and Stephen, took over culinary duties later in the day, with a little help—or otherwise—from Bethany and Eliza. Tim rarely indulged in domesticity, which was something of a relief for the food lovers in the house. Peverill Lodge might officially be a boarding house, but in reality it was home—owned by Rina, it was true, but costs and chores shared equally between all those she counted as kin.

Tim bounded through the door, fully dressed and looking chipper, Rina thought.

'It went well then?' she asked him.

'Of course it did,' Bethany said. 'Tim always puts on a good show.'

Tim beamed. 'Very well,' he agreed. 'Rina, I've been talent spotted, or whatever you call it. Some big London agent called Marcus Price. Do you know him?'

'After my time, dear, but I know the name. So that's why you were late?'

'Yes, we stayed talking in the bar after everything closed. Hopefully the filming will happen at the Palisades.'

'Filming? At the hotel? That should be good for business. What's it all about then?'

'Well.' Tim frowned as though trying to get everything in order in his brain. 'It's a series about buildings that have been brought back to life. Theatres, hotels, that sort of thing. You know how there's been this new wave of heritage-style programmes on TV?'

Rina nodded.

'So not actually about your magic, then?' Bethany sounded disappointed.

'Oh, but it will still be wonderful exposure,' her sister chided. 'Tim, you'll shine anyway.'

'Of course he will,' Bethany agreed. 'Tim, you mustn't be disappointed that it's not all about you. Your break will come, you know.'

'Right,' Tim said, momentarily nonplussed.

'So this is a series,' Rina prompted.

Tim nodded. 'Six parts, each one looking at a different part of the country, but the good thing is, the Palisades would be featured on the Christmas edition.'

Rina looked more closely at her protégé. From the look of barely suppressed excitement on Tim's face, there was more to this. 'And?' she said.

'And . . . it would be going out live. Rina, imagine that. Live television.'

Rina *could* imagine, having done it herself.

'That's quite a risk,' she said. 'Exciting, yes, but—'

'But Tim does his act live every night,' Eliza objected. 'So what can possibly go wrong just because it's going to be on the television? Rina, you are a cold fish sometimes. We think it's wonderful, don't we, Bethany?'

Tom cast an apologetic look in Rina's direction, followed by a tiny shrug, a habit he seemed to have picked up from his fiancée, Joy.

'Oh, I don't doubt Tim will be wonderful,' Rina agreed, 'I'm just wondering how the Palisades will cope with an entire production team. It's really good news, dear. Joy will be delighted.'

Tim nodded enthusiastically and set about helping Rina carry dishes of bacon and sausage to the table, just as the final members of the household made their entrance. The Montmorency twins had performed as a double act for so long that they seemed to have forgotten how to be separate individuals. 'The twins' as they always called themselves—as did everyone else who did not wish to cause mortal offence— could not have looked less identical, though anyone who knew them for any length of time seemed to be drawn into the same conceit and, in Rina's experience, to register only the similarities. In reality, Matthew was tall and rather elegant with his mane of steel grey curls, whereas his eponymous brother was short and slightly round, thinning on top and unlike Matthew in practically every way.

'Any news on *your* project?' Tim asked.

'You mean Rina's relaunch?' Eliza asked.

'Just think,' Bethany added, '*Lydia Marchant Investigates* coming back after all this time.'

'Not that she ever went away,' Matthew put in. 'I mean, the programme has been franchised in, oh, how many countries, Rina? It's on cable and satellite all the time.'

That was true, Rina thought, a fact which contributed to the financial well-being of Peverill Lodge. 'Nothing is fully decided yet,' she reminded them, though there had already been a series of script and scheduling meetings. Discussions centred on the possibility of picking up from where they had left off, and revamping the storylines that had already been submitted for the eleventh series which had never been made. There were some, Rina included, who thought it would be better to go for a complete relaunch. It was, after all, eight years since Lydia Marchant had graced television screens. Rina was alternately hopeful and despairing about it all.

'Not that she ever stopped investigating,' Tim muttered, as though reading her thoughts.

She smiled back at him. 'I'm due to give my agent a call later in the week,' she said. 'Hopefully I'll know a little more then.' She settled to breakfast, Matthew pouring tea and Stephen serving the eggs, the morning ritual establishing itself as it always did. Rina felt a slight moment of disquiet.

'They'll all be fine, even if you have to go away for the filming,' Tim murmured, doing that thought reading thing again. 'And I'll be close by, Mac and Miriam too, and they're not helpless, you know. Just a bit eccentric.'

Rina nodded gratefully, knowing he was right. She was really hoping that Lydia Marchant, her most successful role, would make a comeback. For one thing it would help with the family finances, and for another she really did want to work again. It would be fun; it was what she did and, as a lady now in her sixties, Rina knew she should seize the chance as it was unlikely to be offered again.

She accepted her tea from Matthew and allowed Stephen to load up her breakfast plate. So lucky, she thought, to have good friends and to have been able to offer them all a place of refuge. The world could be cruel to those unable to fend for themselves. She counted herself so fortunate too that Tim, young enough to be her son but also her closest friend these past few years, had decided he would stick around in Frantham even after he moved out of Peverill Lodge. His fiancée had made the decision to come to live with him rather than ask Tim to move north to Manchester, and Rina was looking forward to seeing more of Joy. Her mother, Bridie, was in the process of finding the young couple a house and helping out with the financing of that—Bridie being a woman with a fortune many times that of Tim's income, even if he did now have regular work.

'Is Mac still coming to dinner today?' Stephen asked.

'Yes, Miriam too, though she says she might be a few minutes late. She's shopping with her sister in Exeter.'

'Ah, that will do her good. It's not been easy, has it?'

No, Rina agreed. It had not been easy. The terrible time late last year when Miriam had been almost lost to them had taken some getting over. Miriam had found herself unable to return to work and was now preparing to go back to university to take her Masters. She was much better, much more confident now, but there was still a fragility under stress that Rina knew would take a long time to harden.

'It will be good to see our favourite policeman,' Bethany said. 'It's been at least a week since he came over.'

'Well, this is a busy time of year,' Eliza agreed. 'All of those tourists and their troubles.'

Rina hid a smile. Compared to last year, Mac must have found work a breeze. No murders, no dramas, just the usual baggage of lost children, the odd stolen purse and a couple who had to be rescued from a remote bit of beach when the tide came in. Not that Mac had actually done the rescuing; he'd just called the coastguard and organized things, but it had been a rare bit of drama in a so far very peaceful summer. Rina figured that the more settled routine had been influential in Mac's decision to stay on in Frantham as the local DI. Earlier in the year he had been very close to quitting. The excuse he'd used for changing his mind was that with Miriam going back to study they needed a steady income, but Rina knew that was only part of the truth, as a friend with a private security firm had offered Mac a well-paid position. Rina had the feeling Mac's reticence was purely down to the fact that he couldn't handle any further changes just now. He'd had enough to last him for a while. He needed routine, familiarity and a little peace, and so far this summer he had managed all of the above.

* * *

While the Martin household was having breakfast, their favourite policeman was leaning on the promenade railing, drinking coffee from the little Italian coffee shop close to the tiny police station and thinking how good life felt.

Strictly speaking, DI Sebastian MacGregor was a little overqualified to be running this substation of policing at Frantham on Sea. He knew full well that this posting was almost the equivalent of gardening leave; that he and his predecessor DI Eden had been sent here because in theory they could neither do harm nor become embroiled in anything that might cause them stress or pain. It was perceived by the powers that be as almost early retirement, but without the paperwork.

Mac had been sent here because he was broken. Events had conspired to tear him apart: the death of a child he could not prevent, the aftermath of a disastrous investigation, then sick leave, mental breakdown and very slow recovery. DI Eden, he now knew, had a similar history, though they had never really spoken about it. Eden had served out his final years here and, so far as Mac could tell, had spent them pretty much as he now spent his official retirement: sea fishing and drinking coffee. Mac's hope of peace and quiet had, at first, been completely scuppered. For a few months it had seemed as though Frantham, backwater that it was, had become crime capital of the world, but it had soon tired of all the drama and settled back into sleepiness.

This summer had been glorious. Sunny, but with a fresh breeze off the sea and a healthy population of visitors, Frantham basked in self-satisfaction and Mac basked with it. He watched the families that had come early to the beach settle on the sand with their buckets and spades. He had noticed that it was those with the youngest infants who turned up earliest; those with older children usually arrived in the afternoon, though there were less of those now, much of the country having already returned to school as September began. The day was warm, and tots in multi-coloured shorts and T-shirts scampered about on the sand or braved the shallows to wet their feet and screech at the cold. Not that it was ever particularly warm, Mac thought. The water here was not so deadly freezing as off the North Sea coast where he had grown up and lived for most of his adult life, but it was still pretty chilly, and it was usually afternoon before tourists—all but the hardiest of them anyway—braved full immersion.

Sipping his coffee, savouring the scent of vanilla syrup, he turned from the railing and wandered back along the promenade towards the police station. The small, square, squat little building, its wooden doors now open wide above the short flight of stone steps and newer, ugly concrete ramp, looked content in the morning light. The red bricks glowed and Mac fancied he could almost hear it stretch and sigh. He laughed at himself, decided he was getting overly sentimental in his old age, but he did feel happy today. Miriam had gone off into Exeter to meet her sister and she had driven herself. This was the first time this year that she had felt able and confident enough to walk up the hill from their home in the boathouse, get into her car and travel the road, alone, that had been the scene of her kidnap. She had called him twice, once just before she had set off and the second time when she had arrived at her sister's place. She had sounded shaky but elated, and Mac had suddenly felt that the entire universe was celebrating with them.

'Morning, Andy,' he said.

'Morning, boss.' The redhead nodded and the freckled face smiled. Andy had not long finished his probationary year.

'Anything happening?'

'One lost dog, one lost purse and a call from DI Kendall,' Andy told him. 'I said you'd get back to him as soon as you got in. It sounded important.'

'But you didn't take a message.'

'But he didn't *leave* a message.' Andy grinned at his boss. 'I did ask. He said it was about an old friend.'

'Friend?'

'Well, friend with imaginary inverted commas,' Andy clarified. 'Anyway, the number's on your desk so you don't have to root for it.'

'Thanks. Where's Frank?' Sergeant Baker usually manned the desk at this time of the morning while Andy sat in the broom cupboard of a back office and dealt with any paperwork.

'He said it was a lovely morning so he'd go and look for the dog,' Andy said. 'You know, the lost one, and that he might think about getting us some of that coffee on the way back.'

Mac laughed and wandered through to his own desk, picking up the phone number Andy had left there and noting, vaguely, that it wasn't either Kendall's mobile or his office number. Frantham was in danger of becoming boringly peaceful, he thought, adding with crossed fingers that he could handle all kinds of boring just now.

It took him a few minutes to get through to his friend and colleague. DI Kendall was, it seemed, at a conference, and the number he had left was the main reception of the hotel.

'We have to keep our bloody phones switched off.' He sounded aggrieved.

'Have I dragged you out of anything important?'

'No, I've left very willingly, and as for important, well I couldn't possibly comment on that one. The only presentation I'm actually here for doesn't happen until tomorrow, but some officious bastard is insisting I attend both days.'

Mac laughed. He had a pretty good idea which conference Kendall had attended, having noticed the memo a few weeks previously. From what he remembered, day one focused on community relations and sensitivity to minority groups. Important, yes, but as Kendall's main expertise was organized crime, and community relations hardly evidenced in his remit, it did seem an odd decision to have tied up a senior officer for both days when day two, relating to the move of organized criminality from an urban to a rural environment, was more truly relevant to Kendall's practice.

'I'm delivering the paper in question,' Kendall said almost apologetically. 'You know I'm doing the MA?'

'I remember you saying.' It seemed everyone was studying these days, Mac thought.

'Yes, well my research is into media representations of crime and how that shapes public response. Actually,' he said almost reluctantly, 'I'm really enjoying it, but, well, you know . . .'

'I know,' Mac agreed, not sure if he actually did. 'What did you want me to call you about, or was it just an elaborate escape plan?'

Kendall laughed. 'Wish I'd thought of it,' he said. 'No, it's about an old acquaintance of ours. Stan Holden. You know he was released?'

'Yes, Rina told me.'

'Right, well it seems time served on remand counted against his sentence. In the end his shooting of Coran was ruled self-defence anyway and the time served counted against the other charges.'

Kendall didn't sound too happy about that, Mac thought.

'So—'

'So we have reason to think he may head your way. He's been living in a hostel since his release, but he left three days ago and he's been in the wind ever since. Just thought you ought to have the heads up, you know.'

Mac could hear someone in the background calling Kendall's name. His friend groaned. 'I'm going to have to go,' he said. 'So much for the escape plan. Oh, you know Rina Martin's been visiting him in jail, I suppose?'

'Yes, she told me that too.'

'Right, well, let her know. Just in case he turns up on her doorstep.'

'I will,' Mac promised. Kendall rang off and Mac was left to reflect that it was very, very likely that Stan would turn up on Rina's doorstep. In fact the only surprise was that he had not already done so. Mac also knew that Kendall would never be able to get his head around the idea that she would welcome him; it would be far too alien a concept for Dave Kendall. In fact, Mac reflected, it was probably the combined influence of eighteen months of Frantham and almost that of Rina that made it seem normal, expected even, for a convicted criminal with Stan's violent past to seek sanctuary in Peverill Lodge.

He wandered back through to the front office, thinking about the routine paperwork waiting on his desk and about Stan Holden. If it hadn't been for Stan then Joy, Tim's young fiancée, would not be with them. She would be dead, just like her brother and father. As would two very innocent little girls. Against those facts, Stan's previous conduct paled, not exactly into insignificance, but, well it kind of balanced things up, Mac thought. He shook himself mentally; that sounded far too much like Rina logic, not the sort of ideas an officer of the law should have floating around in his head.

Sergeant Baker bustled in through the big double doors, his round face reddened by the summer sun and the remnants of sunburn now flaking from his balding scalp. He smiled broadly. 'Lovely morning,' he said. 'Lovely. I thought

I'd take a drive up to the De Barr hotel and a bit of a walk along the cliff path, show some presence, you know?'

Mac nodded. 'Sounds like a good idea,' he approved. Frank Baker was popular with the summer visitors, always ready for a chat, his broad-shouldered, uniformed presence seeming to epitomize what most visitors expected in a rural policeman. 'On your way back, swing round by the aerodrome, will you, make sure they've got everything settled for the open day.' The rather lovely art deco tower and tiny airport were now almost fully restored and had been operational for several months. The impact on local jobs had already been a positive one and the official opening was only a couple of weeks away.

'Will do.'

'I'm out at the Palisades this morning,' Andy reminded him, referencing the larger hotel out towards the Exeter road where Tim performed. 'Security check?'

'Oh yes, so you are. No problem, I can hold the fort here. If there's a sudden crimewave I'll give one of you a call.'

He watched them depart, chatting amicably as they left through the main doors and then round to the awkward little parking space at the back of the police station. Mac stood on the doorstep, sipping the remnants of his coffee and gazing out on to the promenade, suddenly glad to be alone. Despite the peace and stability of his surroundings, he found he had a lot to think about. Everything in his life seemed about to change again. Miriam was going back to university to finish her long-put-off postgraduate studies—Mac was helping her to finance them and was still shocked at the cost. She was talking about her PhD and speculating that it would probably take her a further four years. She'd already had a chat with a potential supervisor and tentatively proposed an area of study in the osteo-archaeology that had been her area of expertise before she had become a CSI. Mac hoped this was the right path for her and that she wasn't just taking flight into academia in response to the events of the previous winter. He wanted to support her, wanted for them both to get it right, and they'd talked the figures through: if they stayed living in the boathouse and Mac continued with his job and Miriam did a bit of part-time work—the nature of which was as yet unspecified—then they would be fine.

She had been worried, he knew, that he'd resent supporting her both emotionally and financially, but he had honestly been able to tell her that he would not. Miriam was one of the best things that had ever happened to him. Rina and her strange family were another. All of that was fine. More than fine. And the fact that he still woke in the night gripped with fear and drenched in a cold sweat was only because he counted Miriam so highly.

She knew about that, of course. It seemed to Mac that sometimes the pair of them took it in turns to be overwhelmed by what might have been.

She understood *that* kind of fear, but what Mac could not admit, was too proud and too embarrassed to admit, was another fear that had crept up on him. What if she found this new life of hers more interesting? What if she met other people, far more suited to her intellect and personality than Mac believed he was?

Most of the time, Mac was able to tell himself that he was being utterly irrational. Miriam would be coming home to him every night, and it wasn't as if she was going away to study. He'd never dream of wanting or trying to stop her from doing anything that made her happy, but that didn't stop the nag of fear that now woke him in the night as often as the memory of almost losing her had done.

'You are such a prize prat,' Mac told himself as he stared out across the promenade. He smiled, deciding he needed Rina to give him a good talking to.

* * *

It had been several days before Jerry had been able to get away from the crowd and make a personal call using a landline—a phone box he had spotted one night when he'd been

20

out at the pub with Santos and the others. It took him a while to get through and he came straight to the point.

'Who set us up? And why haven't the police gone public?'

There was a slight pause. 'Where are you? Can you talk?'

'No time, I'll be missed. You know what a tight rein he keeps. So what the hell is going on?'

'Interpol tell us it wasn't a police operation. Intel suggests it was Vaschinsky. Beyond that I've got nothing to tell you.'

'Right.' Jerry thought for a moment. 'I want out,' he said. 'Now.'

The slight hesitation again. 'Your cover?'

'Still intact so far as I can tell. But I want out. Now. There's nothing to stop me just walking away.'

'No, there's not, except you know he'd find you. And her. Jerry, another week, two at most, then we'll talk. Can you cope with that?'

Jerry hung up. 'Don't have much frigging choice, do I?' he said.

THREE

On Tuesdays, twice a month in the tourist season, there was a small art and antique market in Charmouth, partly in the village hall but also spreading into the little car park and along the pavement. Rina liked to visit—occasionally she liked to buy—and then to enjoy a walk along the fossil beach. She loved Lyme Regis too, having collected fossils as a little girl and now returning to it in a small way so much later in her life, but Charmouth beach was generally a bit less crowded and also a tad easier on the feet. Although it was only a mile or so along the coast, it was unusual to find Jurassic remnants at Frantham; the old town, snuggled into a small crack in the cliffs that followed the outfall of a fast-flowing stream, didn't have a beach, and the sandy, shingly mix of the beach in Frantham new town, the Victorian build, was surprisingly fossil free. Rina suspected that the Jurassic seam dived down underground at that point; either that or something in the geology made it unfit for preservation.

The art and antique fair didn't open until eleven and when Rina arrived people were still setting up. She knew most by sight and a few by name and waved a greeting as she passed by on her way to the beach. The day was shaping up to be a hot one, she thought; it would be good to get down to where there was likely to be a sea breeze.

'Morning, Rina.'

She turned with a smile, recognizing the voice. 'Good morning, Harry. Find anything interesting?'

'This morning, no. It's been too dry, but I came down a couple of days ago after that bit of a squall, big chunk of cliff had slipped during the night. Found some nice bits and pieces the next morning.'

'Good for you. Well, I'm just going to have a bit of a firkle before the antique thing opens.'

'Right you are then, hope you find something nice.'

She could feel him watching her as she walked away, wondering if there was something wrong. Rina sighed. Ordinarily she'd have stopped and chatted with Harry, asked him about his fossil finds and his family and exchanged a bit of gossip. Somehow she didn't have the heart for it this morning; she needed time with her own thoughts. Rina was not someone given to moroseness, but she seemed to be experiencing a real attack of it at the moment and she didn't like the feeling very much.

Rina wasn't sure what had brought it on, but she seemed to be suffering from a terrible attack of *might-have-beens*. A sort of false nostalgia for events that might have happened in her life if things had been different. It annoyed her, but at the same time she found she couldn't help herself.

'You need a change of scene and a change of pace,' she told herself sternly. 'This is no good for anyone, Rina Martin, so stop it right now.'

Unexpectedly, tears pricked at her eyes. She felt in her bag for a tissue and surreptitiously wiped them away. Just what was this all about? True, she was sad about the prospect of Tim leaving Peverill Lodge, but she knew both he and Joy would be frequent visitors, and though it wouldn't be the same, she was genuinely happy about Tim's relationship and loved Joy dearly. Maybe it was the thought that her career might not really be about to get a new lease of life. Maybe that was it—she was afraid of the disappointment?

A small boy hurtled past her, heading towards the sea, sister and mother in hot pursuit. They were laughing. Rina watched as they splashed in the shallows, jumping over the lazy little waves. She watched them with something verging on hunger. We could have had children, she thought. Fred would have made a wonderful father, and she didn't think she'd have done too badly in the maternal stakes either. After Fred had died so suddenly only five years into their marriage, Rina had given up on any ideas of motherhood. She'd known instinctively that she'd never find anyone like Fred again. That she'd never fall in love so completely and utterly. And she'd been right, hadn't she? There'd never been another man who could take his place.

'Not that I ever looked very hard,' she muttered, dabbing at her eyes again and telling herself that it was the unexpectedly strong wind coming in off the sea that was causing her eyes to water.

Determinedly, she turned and began to walk along the beach close to the water's edge, looking for fossils or anything interesting that might have been washed out of the cliffs. Once she'd found a little geode, smashed in half and with bright white crystals inside. Mostly it was just ammonites or lumps of iron pyrite.

Would Tim and Joy have children?

Rina was pretty sure they would, in time. Bridie would be a doting grandmother and Rina a loving surrogate aunt. It was a good thought.

On that more optimistic note she turned back towards the village. She'd go and forage among the art and antiques for a bit, see which new artists had brought their wares to sell and if any of the regular traders had anything worth buying. Rina knew most of it was tat, but as the inhabitants of Peverill Lodge had something of a penchant for pretty china and unusual glassware, there was often something to be had.

* * *

Mac worked his way through the day's paperwork and the interdepartmental emails that seemed to multiply week by week. Most were irrelevant to the small team at Frantham, but he made a point of looking at them anyway, telling himself that it helped him keep track of what was going on in the wider world. A part of Mac had already resigned itself to spending the rest of his career at Frantham, followed by a quiet send off and peaceful retirement—despite the fact that retirement was actually years away. Yet at the back of his mind was the thought he might one day want a more demanding life. The past eighteen months had seen Mac involved in unexpectedly major investigations and he'd got to admit that, once he'd dealt with the fear of failure, and allowing for the more personal threats to himself and Miriam, he'd actually enjoyed the challenges.

The day brought up to date, he fetched Stan Holden's file and sat down to flick through the pages. He was familiar with Holden's career: its trajectory from armed forces to organized crime. Having spoken to him on a number of occasions, Mac could understand how this man, cast adrift from what had once been his life in the army, had been unable to reintegrate. He knew also that Stan was piercingly honest about his life and the choices he had made. He expected no pity and he made no excuses. Odd as it may sound, Stan had a very strong moral compass; that didn't necessarily mean that his magnetic north was the same as the rest of the world's.

And now he was coming back here, as Mac had always known he would. Would he reoffend? Not if Rina Martin had anything to do with it, Mac thought, but statistics were against them both in this case.

Mac sighed and closed the file. Hope for the best, he thought. Prepare for the worst—that was all he could do.

* * *

'Rina, m'dear. Glad you turned up today, I've got something you might like.'

Ted Eebry was one of Rina's favourite stall holders. An inveterate collector of ephemera, he often had bits and bobs of a theatrical nature that Rina bought from him. This time, though, he had more than the odd playbill. From beneath the floor-length cloth covering his stacked table he produced a cardboard box and then a second.

'What on earth do you have there?' Rina laughed. 'Ted, whatever it is, I'll never get it on the bus.'

He kicked out a chair from behind his table and set the boxes down. 'Take a look,' he said. 'If you think you might be interested I can drop them off at home for you so you can get a proper look. Then we can settle on a price.'

Rina eased open the dusty cardboard boxes, curious as to the treasure that might lurk inside. 'Where did you get this lot?' she asked, withdrawing a stack of programmes and fly-ers and press cuttings. Most seemed to date from the 1960s, though as she delved deeper into the box, she seemed to be delving back through the years.

'My son-in-law does house clearance. He turned up with these a couple of nights ago. Thought they might be of interest and once I'd had a quick look I thought of you.' He turned away to attend to a customer and Rina opened one of the programmes she had picked up. She knew these names: the performers and even the impresario. She had worked with two or three of them in the early days. Those pretty girls smiling out at her had sung on the same stage. She remem-bered them. Now what would she have been doing . . . ? Rina smiled. In her long career she'd done it all: touring theatres, knife throwers, and even a comedy dance act with a man dressed as a chicken—though she preferred to forget Jock the Rooster and his Chickadees . . .

'Up your street?' Ted asked her.

'Oh, I rather think they are, thank you, Ted. Did your son-in-law say who they'd belonged to?'

'I don't know that I asked him. I will though. Right, well I'll get them dropped in to you tomorrow or the night after, you can take a rummage and then we'll sort it out from there.'

Rina thanked Ted and helped him tuck the boxes back under the table. Most people would have just thrown them out, she thought. Just a couple of boxes full of old junk. But it would be fun to wallow for a while. Leaving Ted to his customers she wandered on, mooching around the stalls and picking out odd bits and pieces she knew the Peters sisters would admire. Bethany was fond of chintz-patterned pottery and Eliza did like her blue glass. Finally, her purchases stowed away, she decided it was time to head for home.

It would be so much easier, she thought, if she could drive. That would save Ted having to drop off her parcels, it would mean she could wander further afield, and if she did get the new Lydia Marchant series off the ground, then it might prove very useful. She had, she realized, come to rely a great deal on Tim to take her about, and though she knew he would always be willing, that was going to become far more difficult as time went on and Joy moved down.

Right, she decided as she boarded the bus headed for home, that's what she would do. It wasn't that Rina couldn't drive—she'd learnt years before and owned a car until moving to Frantham—it was more a case of her never having really enjoyed the process. She could book some refresher lessons, she decided. Find herself a nice, sympathetic, patient instructor and get driving again, then get a little car.

Oddly satisfied that she'd decided on a course of action, Rina told herself that this was exactly what she needed. Some sort of focus, something to offset that unfortunate tendency towards moroseness that seemed to be overtaking her and which was bringing to her attention a Rina Martin she almost did not recognize.

* * *

Karen had watched him arrive at the restaurant. She knew his routine and it was an exemplar of his arrogance and confidence that he should be such a creature of habit. That same restaurant every Tuesday lunchtime. Usually he dined alone—apart from the driver and one of his bodyguards.

Alonso's was a family-run place. Not particularly posh or particularly big, but comfortable and welcoming and Karen could attest to the quality of the food. She waited until he'd been settled at his usual table and then sashayed across the road and went inside, a brown Manila envelope clasped tightly in her hand.

'Mr Vaschinsky is expecting me,' she told the waiter who approached her and asked if she was dining alone. The waiter looked slightly puzzled, but used to their patron's slightly odd habits, he left Karen and went over to the table set apart in the little alcove at the back.

Vaschinsky frowned, began to deny that he was expecting anyone. Then looked up and saw who it was. She watched as his expression changed and his face flushed and then grew pale. He wasn't pleased to see her, then?

Karen took a deep breath as she crossed the restaurant. Eight months ago Vaschinsky had decided she was surplus to requirements, and she was taking a terrible risk coming here, even if it was a very public place. No one would blink should he order one or other of his men to take her out the back and finish what they were supposed to have done back then.

Talk fast, she told herself, and say all the words he wants to hear.

Vaschinsky motioned for Karen to sit down and handed her a menu. So he'd decided to be amused, she thought. So far, so good. She handed the envelope to one of Vaschinsky's men. He looked at his boss, who nodded, then he ripped it open.

Karen studied the menu. The waiter, she noticed, had made himself scarce.

The man with the big mitts that she'd given the envelope to was going through the papers. He wouldn't understand them, she thought, not entirely, but he'd get the gist.

'Boss?'

He handed the package to Vaschinsky, who read in silence for a minute or two.

'So,' he said, shuffling the paperwork together and tucking it back into the envelope. 'And what do you want in return?'

'Time in Frantham. I've things to do. I don't want to be looking over my shoulder while I'm doing them.'

'Time.' He steepled his fingers together. 'You're taking a great risk, Karen Parker. I could have you killed right here and now.'

'You could, but that would spoil your lunch,' Karen said.

'Oh, I don't know.' He frowned. 'It seems to me that some of the finer details, account numbers and the like, are missing?'

Karen nodded. 'When I've finished what I need to do, I'll give you the rest,' she said. 'Like I said, I just need some time.'

'To do what?'

'Oh, kill a couple of people and make sure my kid brother's OK. Things like that.'

'And why are you doing this? What do you have against Haines?'

Karen shrugged. 'You want what Haines has; I need you off my back. It seems logical. It's nothing particularly personal against Haines, just payment for safe passage.'

Vaschinsky nodded. 'And the killing part?'

Karen smiled slightly. 'Ah,' she said. 'Now that *is* personal.'

She could almost hear Vaschinsky thinking, weighing up what she had given him and what he might hope to gain. Discovering that she had been the one to provide the intel on the French debacle—and she knew he had profited greatly from that—would both amuse and possibly annoy him. Vaschinsky didn't like freelancers, not unless he was paying them, and she'd blotted her copybook there.

'Two weeks,' he said. 'I'll give you two weeks of, as you say, free passage. After that, either you are gone from my sight or it is open season. You understand me?'

Karen nodded. 'Thank you, Mr Vaschinsky,' she said. She handed the menu back and stood up. 'Enjoy your meal. Gentlemen.'

She managed to hold it together until she'd crossed the street and put what she reckoned was sufficient distance between herself and the men in the restaurant, then the shakes began. Karen bent over, retching painfully, and was violently sick in the gutter.

God, the things I do for you, Georgie boy, Karen thought. Though not just for George, she had to admit. Some things just brought their own satisfaction.

FOUR

Stan hadn't been sure at first that it was her; she'd changed her hair colour again—dark now, whereas in the only pictures he'd seen of her she'd been blonde. She'd let it grow as well and wore it tied back in a low ponytail. She was dressed in a blue denim skirt and pale T-shirt, summer sandals on her feet and a brightly coloured bag slung over her shoulder. Playing the tourist, are we? Stan thought, realizing suddenly that he was oddly unsurprised that she was here.

He was aware that she'd spotted him too, and when she smiled and gestured towards a nearby café he followed her. He and his team had once been tasked with getting rid of this girl, Haines kidding himself that this would be an easy disposal and hoping to gain kudos with some fellow called Vaschinsky. Even then Stan had suspected it would not be straightforward, and so it had proved.

They perched like a couple of kids on high stools and the young woman giggled.

'Fancy seeing you here.'

'Fancy,' he agreed. 'I thought you'd be long gone.'

'I was, then I came back, I went away again, and now . . .'

'Now you're back to see that brother of yours?'

31

'To see,' she agreed, 'not to be seen.'

'Oh?'

She dismissed the question with a shrug and ordered for both of them. Some kind of fruit concoction for herself and a tea for him.

'What is that thing?' he asked.

'Mango, peach, lots of crushed ice. I heard you were out. Going to Rina's, are you?'

'Maybe. I've not decided yet.'

'Yeah, right.' She laughed. 'I don't think I'll be paying a visit this time. I sort of blotted my copybook the last time I was here.'

'So I heard. So, what are you here for? And don't tell me it's coincidence we ran into one another.'

She prodded a straw into her drink and eased round in her seat so she could look out at the sparkling ocean. 'Not entirely a coincidence, no. I mean, I'd not actually planned on seeing you today, but I thought we might run into one another sooner or later. It's sort of inevitable, isn't it?'

She smiled and Stan felt a chill run down his spine. She was what, twenty? Twenty-one? A slight, slim, pretty little thing, and yet another that could answer the subtle-as-a-knife description Coran would have used.

Dangerous, Stan thought, and with none of the usual sense of caution that might slow her down.

'And you?' she asked. 'You're here for Haines.'

It wasn't a question.

Stan shrugged. 'I've not made up my mind yet.'

She laughed, and for an instant Stan could almost imagine she was normal. Her laugh was genuine and the way it made her eyes dance and the corners crinkle utterly real and true. Stan understood all too well how people might be fooled, but he knew better than that. He'd seen what she was capable of and heard about a lot more besides.

'So, what are you calling yourself now?' he asked. 'Still Karen Parker?'

'Oh, I'm sticking with Karen,' she said. 'It's a common enough name. But I'm Munroe now, Karen Munroe, and don't worry, Stan, I'm not about to get in your way. I think we've got a cause in common here, don't you?'

Stan sipped his tea and watched her smile. This time it didn't reach her eyes.

* * *

'Stop, stop, stop!' Elodie waved her arms and jumped up and down. The digger stopped and the engine cut out. The driver climbed down from his cab and came over to where she stood.

'Spotted something?' Joe asked.

'More bones, I think. I just caught a glimpse.'

She pointed at the spoil heap and Joe frowned. 'We neither of us saw anything last night,' he said. 'I've only tipped one bucket load today.'

'I know. It was when you dropped the new soil on top. Something moved.'

They climbed down into the ditch at the base of the soil heap and Elodie crouched down, hands delving carefully into the loose earth. Joe watched avidly. He had known nothing much about archaeology before she had come on site. The local authority had sent in a routine team to check up on the access road into the newly refurbished flight field. Ten years back some bits of pottery had been found by field walkers, so the law said archaeologists had to be given access to the site.

Archaeologists—three of them—had come and gone, deciding there was little of interest, and Elodie, a post-grad student, had been left behind to keep an eye on things. Three days ago they had uncovered bones. Human bones. Work had been halted and Joe and his digger sent to clear out the old drainage ditches surrounding the flight field, which should, theoretically, have had nothing new to show anyone.

The three more important archaeologists had returned and Elodie was sent off to keep an eye on Joe and his excavations.

Not, he thought, that she seemed to mind. And he certainly didn't. Blonde, tanned, lithe and vibrant—he thought Elodie was gorgeous.

Joe squatted down beside her. 'There's not supposed to be anything over this way,' he said. 'The drainage ditches have been cleared out regularly, haven't they?'

Elodie shrugged. 'I don't know,' she said. 'The records for the site are a bit patchy, but I definitely saw something.' She frowned and dug her hands back into the crumbly earth.

'Are you sure that's the stuff I just dug out?' Joe said. 'It looks too dry.'

'Dry?' She sat back on her heels and looked. 'Dry,' she repeated. 'It shouldn't be dry.'

'No, look, the last bucket load is there, see. Black and wet and full of organic matter.' He was quite proud of that phrase.

Elodie laughed. 'Organic matter,' she mocked.

'Yeah, you know, dead leaves and muck.' He fell back laughing as she pushed him off balance.

'Hey, who's supposed to be the expert round here?'

'Expert, eh? I thought the only experts on site were over by the bones on the new road. I don't see any expert here, just some lowly post-grad student stuck up to her ankles in mud in a drainage ditch.'

She shoved at him again and he caught her hand, dragged her down beside him, then pulled her very close. She smelt wonderful, he thought. Floral perfume blended with sun-warmed skin and the rich, loamy scent of fresh-turned earth. He kissed her hungrily, then let go reluctantly as she pulled away.

'Bones,' she said. 'Save that for later, OK?'

Later, Joe thought, grinning at her like an idiot. 'Promise?'

'Promise, now help me look.'

Gently, they began to sift through the soil. It crumbled between their fingers, fell away dry as they touched it. 'This is all wrong,' Elodie said, and Joe knew she was right.

'Look.' He pointed at a small fragment of white protruding from the loose fill. Elodie brushed at it, uncovering a fragment a couple of inches long.

'Is that what you saw?'

She shook her head. 'No, I swear I saw a long bone.' She placed the fragment in one of the plastic trays they used for finds and then dug deeper, gently brushing the earth aside, layer by layer. 'There.'

Definitely a long bone, Joe thought; he'd seen several this past week. 'A tibia?' he guessed.

'Well, listen to you.' She frowned. 'These don't look right.'

'They don't look like the other bones,' Joe agreed. The first ones they'd found had been pitted and friable, and darker than this, stained with all the years of being buried in the earth. By contrast, these looked fresh, pale and very solid, unmarked but for a few . . . well, what looked to Joe like shallow cut marks. He pointed them out. 'What's that there?'

With her forefinger, Elodie gently examined the marks. Deeper than scratches, very straight, very deliberate. Almost reverently she placed the bone in the tray beside the shorter fragment. 'I don't think this is archaeology,' she said finally. 'Joe, I think we need to get some advice on this. I don't think we should touch anything else.'

He agreed. He'd been intrigued by the earlier finds. The dead of a couple of thousand years ago, reverently laid to rest, their interment accompanied by care and ritual, but this filled him with a different emotion. Bones tumbled into a ditch and covered with loose earth that had, he felt, almost certainly not come from the scene. This was definitely not the same.

He took her hand and they scrambled out of the ditch, then turned to look back at the pile of earth. The scrape from the digger bucket was clear and defined, as was the blackened mud he had excavated just a few minutes ago. At first glance the friable earth further down at the side of the spoil heap looked like dried and crumbled soil from the day before, and he could now see where some of the previous day's mud had been piled up to cover it. Unfortunately for whoever had practised such concealment, the load Joe had dropped on to the heap that morning had caused the loose pack to slide, exposing the foreign soil.

'I don't like this, Elodie.' He glanced around as though suddenly afraid that whoever had dumped the bones and earth was still there, watching them. Not more than a hundred yards away the rest of the team worked and voices, machines, the sounds of tools, metal on metal, clear and familiar, drifted across. Those sounds did nothing, Joe thought, to dispel the sudden sense of unease.

'We'd best report this,' he said and he felt her nod. The way things were going here, he didn't see the new access road being ready for the open day.

* * *

It happened that PC Andy Nevins was the first officer on the scene. Neither Andy nor Frank Baker being at the police station, Mac hadn't felt able to leave. He had called Frank, who had still been up on the cliff top on foot, so Mac had summoned Andy.

'They've found some bones at the dig,' he said.

'Isn't that what they're supposed to find on a dig?'

'These are different, apparently. Check it out will you, Andy, see if we need to call in the big guns.'

And so Andy Nevins was now on his knees, peering into a ditch with Elodie on one side of him, Joe on the other, and three more senior archaeologists looking on.

Work had stopped across the site and the foreman had summoned the owner of the airfield. Edward de Freitas was now on his way.

'What do you think?' Elodie demanded. 'It doesn't look right, does it?'

Andy was inclined to agree. 'Um, what do they think?' he asked, nodding towards the other archaeologists.

'Oh, they agree. This isn't archaeology, this is something else. Look, you can see where we've hit the natural clay level there. The ground is clean, no sign of anything, and this ditch has been cleaned out God knows how many times. The other bones we found were what we'd expect on a site like this: crouched burials, with grave goods. The condition of the bones was pretty poor, but you could see how they'd been laid out, and the remnants of their grave goods.'

'I saw the pictures in the paper.' Andy nodded. He sat back on his heels. 'These are certainly not old bones,' he decided, 'and I think you're right, someone's dumped them here and then covered them up with . . . well, it looks like garden compost.'

'That's what we thought,' Joe agreed.

Andy stood up and brushed off his knees. 'Got to call the boss,' he said. 'I think we need the CSIs and someone a bit more senior than me to deal with this one.' He paused, staring at his mobile phone for a moment as the thought seized him that he might be able to persuade Mac to let him carry on here for a bit. Life for the newly qualified PC Nevins hadn't been nearly as interesting as life for probationer Nevins had proved to be. He could do with a bit of a challenge. He dialled Mac's number and began to fill him in on what was happening. 'Oh, hang on, boss, Edward de Freitas has just arrived. You want a word?'

'You're on scene, Andy. You can tell him more than I can. I'll have a word after you've briefed him, if he wants one. Meantime, I'll get on to SOCO and I'll call and tell Frank not to hurry himself. I'm sure you can manage.'

'OK, will do,' Andy signed off. He could feel himself blushing as he always did when stressed or happy, the knowledge that Mac thought he was well able to cope with the situation creating both reactions simultaneously.

Edward de Freitas was crouching down where Andy had knelt. Andy joined him. 'Mac is sending the CSIs,' he said.

'Good.' Edward frowned. 'Do we know what's down there yet?'

'No, not really. Elodie and Joe spotted the bones. They realized pretty quickly that something was wrong and preserved the scene after that.'

'But the bones are human?'

'They think so, yes.'

Edward stood up. 'So what do you want us to do?' he said. 'Do we need to close the whole site?'

Andy thought about it. He glanced around, appraising the position of the site in relation to the road and the airfield and what facilities were available. He knew Edward de Freitas quite well, having worked an earlier case that had involved him, and knew he could rely on the older man's cooperation.

'OK,' he said, 'I think if we could keep those barriers next to the road in place, route all site traffic back through the old entrance, then the CSI team and anyone else we bring in can come round the back and get to the scene through that gap in the hedge. Joe tells me only he and Elodie came along that bit of road this morning and everyone else has cut across from the Portakabin and the actual dig, so I think we can assume only Elodie and Joe have come the way of whoever dumped the bones. If we can close off from the barriers to the trackway and that bit of verge, the rest of the site can carry on as normal.'

Edward nodded. 'OK, whatever you need to do. I'll go and talk to the site foreman, tell him what's happening and that you may need extra pairs of hands, and can I suggest we move one of the vans down to the end of the lane to act as a temporary road block? The media are bound to get wind of this and if we can keep them on the verge near the main road it'll make your life a whole lot easier.'

Andy hadn't thought of that. 'Thanks,' he said. What else? He had an odd feeling that Edward de Freitas had already thought of the 'what else', but was waiting, almost willing Andy to come up with it himself. He took a look around. There was a gap in the hedge where the new slip road was due to go through, and the little bridge that would take traffic over the drainage ditch that Joe and Elodie had been clearing had been marked out. On the other side of the hedge the airfield had its own security patrols, there initially while the building work had been going on to protect the site and the materials left there. The main gate, allowing access on to the road into Frantham, was currently padlocked while the building work was finished, public access allowed only via the stile and—

The public footpath. Of course.

'Would it be possible to get your security people to set up a permanent station that side of the fence to keep an eye on anyone coming down from the coastal path? We can arrange a cordon, but having someone on site would be really helpful. Unless this escalates into a murder enquiry, I don't know how many extra bodies I can call upon.'

Edward de Freitas nodded and Andy felt a glow of satisfaction that he'd not had to be prompted further. 'I'll go and see to that now,' he said. 'Let me know if there's anything further I can do.'

Andy watched him go and felt oddly lonely. He was aware of several pairs of eyes—Elodie, Joe and the archaeologists among them—watching and waiting to see what would happen next and what he was going to do.

Statements, he should get that under way. Find out who had been where and when and construct a timeline for yesterday and this morning.

One of the other workers called out to him. 'Boss says you can use that Portakabin,' he said. 'We're just clearing you some space and getting the kettle on.'

Welcome news, Andy thought. He was lucky this was de Freitas's land. Edward considered that he owed Mac big time and therefore, by extension, was willing to be helpful to his deputy and make sure everything went smoothly.

Deputy, Andy thought. That had a good ring to it.

He knew there were time constraints. The formal opening was only a couple of weeks away, all of the publicity was out and there was a general buzz in the Frantham community about this new boost to the local economy. Andy felt the

39

implicit pressure to get things cleared up quickly, but was relieved not to be reminded overtly for the moment.

'I'll need statements from everyone,' he said. 'And do you have CCTV on site?'

'Not over this side,' Joe told him. 'There's a couple of cameras keeping an eye on the heavy equipment and so on, they feed into the security cameras on the airfield, but there's nothing to look at here. Or there wasn't.'

Andy nodded, slightly disappointed. But, he thought, you never knew, the camera might have caught someone coming on site. He led everyone back to the designated Portakabin. Two tables were covered in plans and maps and the walls decorated with paperwork. A young woman in a high vis jacket was unpinning some kind of schedule and moving it, page by page, to a pinboard close to the stacked tables while her colleague fiddled with a computer set on a now empty desk.

'Boss says you can use this,' he said. He didn't look particularly pleased.

'And there's tea- and coffee-making stuff there,' the woman added. 'Will this give you enough room? Only we're a bit pushed for space.'

Andy assured her it was more than enough. Everyone seemed to have crowded into the doorway behind him and he saw the look of amusement on the woman's face.

'If you could all, um, wait outside,' Andy said, 'I'll get sorted out and get the statements done.'

The man left and the woman drifted off to sort out papers down at the other end of the cabin. After a moment she departed too, awkwardly clutching a rolled up chart, a large hammer and a can of spray paint. Andy wondered what she was planning to do.

Then he was alone. Desk in front of him, computer waiting expectantly and—he could see through the half-open door—an orderly queue of would-be witnesses waiting outside.

Andy's heart suddenly sank. He wished Mac were here to tell him what to organize first, or the round, comfortable presence of Sergeant Frank Baker. What would Baker do?

Come on, lad, he'd say, call the first one in. Start with them as can tell you least on account of them not being around. Get their statements and get rid, then focus on the important folk.

Right, the important folk would be Elodie and Joe, so deal with the archaeologists first, maybe see them as a group and get their take on things, and then take proper statements from Joe and Elodie and have a chat with the site foreman and find out who was last on site.

Happy that he had a plan, Andy found his notebook, opened a file on the computer and called his first witnesses to order.

FIVE

Haines did not like Vaschinsky, but that didn't stop them talking business, even operating together when the situation demanded it. The phone call had come as something of a surprise though; Haines had not expected to hear from his potential business associate for another week or so.

'I hear you had trouble,' Vaschinsky said.

'A little.'

'You lost two men and a couple of million dollars. I think that qualifies as trouble. Tell me, Haines, why do you insist on trading in dollars? What is wrong with pounds sterling?'

Haines frowned but did not rise to the bait.

'I've got some information for you,' Vaschinsky told him. 'I know who tipped off the French authorities. Turns out it was an old acquaintance of ours.'

Haines's frown deepened. 'Who?' he demanded.

Vaschinsky laughed. 'Young Karen Parker,' he said. 'Oh, and I believe she is heading your way.'

Haines lowered the receiver slowly, face like thunder. Jerry, who'd been sitting close enough to hear both sides of the conversation, was wise enough to say nothing.

Not the police, he thought again. He knew that for certain now. So who?

Vaschinsky. He knew about the deal. He knew what had gone wrong. What if he'd set it up? If it had been his people that night?

Haines got stiffly to his feet and left the cabin calling for Santos. Next thing Jerry knew they were headed for port and he'd been tasked with booking a suite and two rooms in some posh hotel he'd never heard of.

'What's going on?' he asked Santos first chance he got.

'You know as much as I do. But he's got the bit between his teeth over something or other. Just remember not to get in his way.'

SIX

Two things interrupted the afternoon routine at Peverill Lodge. One was welcome: Rina's antique dealer friend happened to be passing and dropped off the boxes of memorabilia. The other was not so welcome.

The doorbell rang just as the household was preparing for afternoon tea, a ritual of cakes and tiny sandwiches over which the Peters sisters presided with due ceremony.

'Who on earth could that be?' Eliza wondered. 'Rina dear, are you expecting anyone? Should I get an extra cup?'

Telling her that she was not, Rina went through to the hall just as Matthew and Stephen appeared, carrying trays of cakes and tea through to the dining room. She let them pass before opening the door. The woman standing on her doorstep was not anyone she recognized. Plump, dark and dressed in a navy skirt and pastel shirt, she looked hot and out of sorts. No tights, Rina noted, but what she always classed as office shoes—black patent courts—on rather swollen feet. She was lugging a rather large briefcase.

'Can I help you?'

'I'm looking for Stan Holden,' the woman said. 'I'm Tina Marsh, his probation officer?'

She made a question of that last statement, as though there might be some doubt about it.

Rina processed that information and drew interesting conclusions. She could hear the conversation in the dining room come to a halt and Matthew and Stephen come back out into the hall.

'Everything alright, Rina?'

'It's fine, thank you, Matthew. I'm afraid he's not here, Miss Marsh. He's gone to see about a job.'

'Oh.' The woman looked momentarily nonplussed. 'Do you know how long he'll be? I really do need to check in with him and—' she struggled to glance over Rina's shoulder—'I need to make sure the accommodation is suitable . . .' She trailed off, withering under Rina's stony glance.

'I can assure you,' Rina said, 'Peverill Lodge is eminently suitable.'

Tina Marsh gathered up her job description and wrapped it around herself. 'I'm sure you think that, but you must understand, I am Mr Holden's probation officer and I do need to speak with him.'

'Of course you do,' Rina agreed. 'But as I said, he isn't here and I'm not sure what time he may be back. If you'd give me your number then I'll be sure to get him to ring you. Does it have to be in office hours? Or would you like to give him a mobile number too, seeing as it's quite late in the afternoon?'

The woman scowled at her and produced a card from the depths of the overstuffed briefcase. 'Office hours will do,' she said, then turned on her heel and left.

Rina closed the door and set the card down on the telephone table.

'You lied to her,' Matthew observed curiously.

'Not a lie, Matthew,' Stephen contradicted, 'merely a pre-emptive statement. If Stan told his probation officer that this was his address, then he obviously intends to come here. He's just not arrived yet. When he does, it will no longer be an untruth, will it?'

Matthew nodded. 'It's as well we baked,' he said.

They retreated to the dining room and Rina reflected that she could not recall a time when cake had not been available at Peverill Lodge. She was concerned, though. Stan had spoken to her just before his release and at that point had not been sure what he wanted to do. He'd called her the day he'd been released too and she'd reiterated her offer of somewhere to stay. He'd promised to get in touch but she'd not really been surprised when the promise had not been kept. Stan was not exactly socialized.

It seemed, though, that he'd made up his mind to accept her offer. So where was he?

A little anxious now, she called Mac. He listened as she told him about the call from the probation service and then relayed what Kendall had told him that morning.

'No doubt he'll turn up,' Rina said. 'The question is—'

'What's he been up to in the meantime?' Mac agreed.

* * *

It was late when the front doorbell rang. Rina, in pink dressing gown and comfy slippers, had sat up watching a late film. Matthew and Stephen sat with her. Matthew was reading and Stephen lay back on the sofa with a pair of very large headphones clamped to his ears, listening to Bruch.

Rina opened the door, Matthew hovering protectively behind her.

Stan stood sheepishly on the doorstep. 'I know it's late—' he began.

Rina stood aside. 'You'd best come in then,' she said. 'Your bed's made up and Matthew has saved some dinner for you.'

'How did you know I'd be here tonight?'

'Because your probation officer called round this afternoon. We didn't think you'd risk going missing for long.'

Stan stepped into the hall. Last time he had been here, Rina thought—the first time he had been inside Peverill

46

Lodge—he and Joy had been on the run from some very dangerous men. They'd been wet and cold and desperate for friendly faces.

He wasn't cold this time and he wasn't wet, but one look at his face told Rina that the rest remained the same. He clutched a shopping bag in his hand and wore the same clothes he had been arrested in, but he looked older and more tired.

'Come through to the kitchen,' she said. 'I'll make some tea and you can get some hot food inside you. You need to call this Marsh woman in the morning, get her off your back. I told her you'd been following up a lead on a job, so we'd best get our stories straight on what that might be before you do.'

She saw his shoulders sag slightly, a mix of relief and exhaustion, she thought. He followed her through to the kitchen and settled down in one of the wooden chairs set beside the scrubbed deal table.

'I don't want to bring trouble to your door,' he said.

'Do you think you will?'

'If I stay I might.'

'So might anyone.'

'Rina, I—'

She held up a hand for silence. 'Tomorrow,' she said. 'Tonight you eat and get some sleep, in the morning we'll have a family conference and you can tell us what your worries are. We'll tell you what we plan to do about them.'

Matthew set a plate and cutlery down in front of him. 'I hope it isn't spoiled,' he said. 'I've kept some pudding for you too. What Rina is saying, Stan, is that we don't turn friends away just because they may have brought their problems with them. That isn't what we are. Now eat before it goes cold and I'll see to that tea.'

Stan wolfed the food set before him and they waited until he'd devoured pudding before saying much more. Stephen joined them and they drank tea and chatted about the box of memorabilia they had been sorting through. Easy, contented conversation between friends. Rina could see that Stan was greedily absorbing that too. She wondered what exactly was on his mind and was surprised when he blurted it out.

'I saw Karen,' Stan said.

'Karen?' Stephen recoiled in horror.

'Yes, but don't worry, she's got no intention of coming here or of trying to speak to George. She said she wants to check up on him, but she knows she's got no place in his life now.'

'And you believe her?' Rina asked.

Stan nodded, slowly. 'I do,' he said. 'I think Karen has unfinished business here, but she knows George has to make his own way now. She still loves him though, so she wants to know what he's up to and such.'

'And this business is?'

Stan hesitated and took another massive gulp of tea. 'Haines,' he said at last. 'Rumour said he was back this way, now I know he is. Karen wants him, and so do I.'

Matthew picked up Stan's plate and took it over to the sink. For a minute or so there was silence, broken only by the sound of running water and the overviolent scrubbing of a china plate.

'He's a dangerous man,' Stephen observed at last.

'Like I said, I don't want to bring trouble.'

Matthew turned from the sink. 'He'll know you're out, I suppose.'

'He will, yes.'

'So you think he's a threat. To yourself, I mean?'

'I've been thinking about that,' Stan said. 'I think he's just been waiting until I came back into focus. He's known where I am, known I couldn't do anything to hurt him where I was, and I think he viewed it as a waste of energy and resources to have me hit inside. Now I'm not sure. If I went away, kept clear, then maybe he'd, well, not forget about me, but put me at the bottom of the list.'

'And are you a threat to him?' Rina asked. 'Stan, what do you plan to do?'

Stan shook his head. 'Rina, I'm not sure I know yet. I got out planning revenge. I wanted . . . wanted Haines and his people taken down, not just for my own protection or those they'll hurt next, but just because . . . Karen has a more personal agenda, I suppose, she knows there are people out there who want her dead and gone and Haines could well be on that list if it suits his agenda or there is some profit in it. Her dad was one of his men; he may have had a low opinion of Parker, but his reputation relies on others knowing that a threat to his people is a threat to him. My guess is that Haines wants her dead and gone and I think she figures she should get in first. Me, I don't know. I could live with the threat. I could go away. I could do a lot of things—'

'But Karen could go away. Keep out of reach,' Matthew argued. 'She's good at that sort of thing. Why come back and stir things up?'

Stan shrugged. He'd given that same question a lot of thought and come up with no definitive answers. 'I've not worked that out yet,' he admitted. 'And she didn't say.'

'And meanwhile you are trying to work out what your options are?' Rina nodded. 'It's not in your nature to run, is it?'

'I never have,' he agreed. 'I think I'm too old to start now. But I didn't expect to have Karen in the mix.'

'So perhaps you should stand back and let her get on with it,' Stephen offered. 'That would seem to be a practical solution.'

Amused, Rina observed Stan's look of surprise. 'Stan,' she said, 'I'll show you your room and where everything is. Feel free to make yourself more tea and there's cake and biscuits in the tins over there. I think it's time we got some sleep and in the morning we'll all talk this through. I think Mac should be involved, don't you?'

Stan shook his head vehemently. 'He's a police officer. You think he'll just stand back while I—'

'He's a police officer and a friend and he needs to know, if he doesn't already, that a dangerous man is back on his patch,' Rina told him sternly. A dangerous young woman too, she added silently. 'This Haines caused a lot of trouble for a lot of people last time he was here. I don't imagine he'll have quieted down. Mac needs to be kept informed.'

Feeling better now he was clean and rested, he padded down the three flights of stairs to the kitchen and made himself some tea.

Six fifteen the kitchen clock told him and still no sound of anyone rising. Now what? Stan thought. He prowled the friendly, tidy space, discovering a utility room through one green door, a pantry through another, playbills on the walls advertising the previous occupations of the house's tenants: the Montmorencys during their time as a comedy double act; the Peters sisters perched decoratively on a grand piano; Rina Martin in *The Importance of Being Earnest* and then in her famous role as Lydia Marchant, investigating on the television. A more recent poster for the Palisades hotel featured a picture of Tim Brandon looking dark and mysterious and glamorous against a backdrop of art deco splendour.

Tea in hand he wandered through to the hall, noting that Tim had obeyed Rina's note and bolted the front door. The room nearest the entrance was closed and Stan did not try the door. In contrast, the living room and dining rooms stood open and he wandered through both, admiring the patina of the much-loved old dining table with its oddly mismatched chairs. He tried to guess which belonged to which occupant. The two lighter, balloon backs he decided must belong to the Peters sisters. The upright and very formal Victorian jobs were Matthew's and Stephen's. Rina's carver had been set at the head of the table, and an elaborate dark oak number—with a cushion on the seat—he guessed was Tim's. He paused, noting abruptly that another chair had now been set opposite Tim Brandon's seat. The high, bobbin-turned back spoke of solidity, and the warm glow of the timber evinced a long life and much polishing. He knew at once that this was now his place at the table and it moved him tremendously that they had already both literally and figuratively made a space for him.

The sound of light footsteps on the stairs brought him back into the hall.

Rina smiled. 'I thought you'd already be up.' She nodded at his mug. 'Any more of that?'

Stan grinned. 'I think there might be,' he said.

* * *

Karen stood in the shadows and watched as the residents of Hill House boarded the minibus and set off for school.

She was used to not being seen, and she knew the layout of the house and gardens well, had made a point of knowing ever since her little brother had come to live there after the death of their parents. Karen had always looked after George. Karen had always looked after their mother too, keeping them safe, keeping them moving. Hiding from the abusive husband and father who had died not so far from where she now stood.

Karen felt a pang of guilt that she was not *still* looking after George. Not directly, anyway. But that had largely been George's choice and she tried not to blame him for it.

He was one of the last to emerge, coming out through the big double doors and then dashing back in again to collect a forgotten something. The girl with him rolled her eyes and then stood and waited for him to return. Blonde, slender and, Karen had to admit, very pretty, Karen knew that Ursula was George's best friend at Hill House. And from the way he briefly took her hand when he returned, something more than that now?

Karen was so taken aback that she almost forgot to look properly at her brother. When she did, she was doubly shocked. He had grown! Long limbed and skinny, now tall enough to tower over Ursula, she could not believe how much he had changed in the months since she had last seen him. He had gone from being a child to a young man and she had missed it.

For a moment Karen felt utterly bereft. It was, she thought, almost like a parent missing that moment when their child takes its first steps. George had changed almost beyond recognition. He pushed back the red curls falling across his forehead and laughed at something Ursula said before clasping her hand once again and walking with her to the minibus.

Karen felt that her heart would break. Of course she wanted George to be happy, she wanted that more than anything, but, oh God, they had been so close for such a long time. All of George's childhood, Karen had been there—his support, his confidante, his parent when their own had proved so inadequate.

Karen smiled at the thought. Not done such a bad job there, she told herself, and allowed that small sense of satisfaction to grow and replace the momentary hurt. George was her success story and nothing was going to change that.

The minibus pulled away and she lost sight of it behind the tall trees that bordered the drive. Karen turned and, keeping close to the line of overgrown shrubs that edged the rather scrubby lawn, made her way back on to the cliff path and then back to her car.

* * *

'It'll be OK,' George said. 'I'll be there and so will Cheryl, and if it all gets too much you just walk away and we'll bring you back home.'

Ursula laughed. 'God,' she said, 'I never reckoned either of us would think of this place as home.'

George grinned. Neither had he. He could recall the time he had first come to live at Hill House. Dank, wintry days when he'd hated the place and the only bright thing anywhere had been Ursula's friendship. He'd been almost thirteen then; now they were both close to fifteen and just starting the first year of their GCSE studies.

He dug in his bag and consulted the still unfamiliar timetable. Three days in and Ursula had already committed hers to memory. He groaned as his worst suspicions were confirmed: 'Double maths and then double history.'

Ursula laughed. 'Could be worse.'

54

'How?'

'You could have that cow Tonks for maths. I mean, how did someone like that ever become a teacher? He hates kids, despises teenagers even more, and he stinks when he leans over you as you're trying to work. Bad breath and BO and cigarette smoke. Ugh.' She shuddered elaborately and George laughed. Miss Patel who taught his group for maths was actually OK, or seemed to be so far, and he was getting most of what she was trying to drill into them, which was a welcome change. They had moved about so much when he was a kid that George's education had been at best patchy, and often lessons from his big sister, Karen, substituted for school. Much to his surprise, though, he was being entered for eight GCSEs and everyone was tentatively confident he'd get A to C grades in probably six of those.

There was a momentary pause and George knew what was coming next.

'Do I have to go on Saturday?'

'No. You can tell Cheryl that you just don't want to. No one will make you.'

No one but Ursula herself.

She grimaced. 'I can't do that though, can I? I mean, it's the first time he's been well enough to want to see me for ages. I can't just . . .'

George said nothing.

'You'll come in with me,' she confirmed, and George squeezed her hand and told her that he would. There were times when he was profoundly relieved he had no father to make demands on him, and there was only a garden of remembrance to visit when he wanted to think about his mother. He felt a pang of guilt as he thought how infrequently that was. It was like it was another life and another George back then and he hated being dragged into the past.

'I hate hospitals,' Ursula said. 'And I hate that place even more.'

Again George knew better than to say anything. Sometimes conversations with Ursula were more about the silences than anything else. At least they were when she talked about family. And she only did that when family imposed themselves on her life; it was rarely voluntary.

George had been to psychiatric hospitals. He'd been to ordinary hospitals too, and to refuges and police stations and social service offices and emergency accommodation and cheap B&Bs. Such had made up the landscape of his childhood, so he could sympathize with Ursula's point of view. Her dad had been in a secure unit for most of the time he had known her, only being returned to open hospitals for brief interludes. He made it to a halfway house once, and there had even been tentative—and totally unrealistic—talk about Ursula moving back in with him one day.

Ursula and George had both known this would never happen, whatever their key worker, Cheryl, and other professional optimists might say. Ursula's dad had retreated from the world and George knew there was no kind of road map or mental satnav that was going to bring him back again.

And there was no way Ursula would ever countenance moving in with her mum, even if the authorities would allow it. Ursula's mum had left a long, long time ago. This year she had even forgotten to send a Christmas card.

The minibus halted to drop the twins off. In their final year at primary school, they were the youngest kids at Hill House. Two of the others that had been there when George arrived, Grace and Richard, had left, moving into bedsits in Exeter now they were both seventeen. Theoretically this was supported accommodation, but George wasn't convinced. He didn't want to think about the time when he and Ursula would have to leave the relative security of the tatty old Victorian pile up on the cliff top.

The others on the minibus were all at the same school as Ursula and George, and a few minutes later they were dropped off in the pedestrian area just a short walk from school, the road immediately outside always being so crowded with buses and parents depositing their kids.

'You OK?' he breathed as they reached the gates and prepared to go to their separate home rooms.

'Yeah, I guess so. Good luck with the maths.'

George grinned. 'Have fun with Tonks.'

She grimaced and walked away.

* * *

Mac had not expected a visit from Rina that morning, and certainly not expected her to be accompanied by Stan. He hid his surprise and bid them both welcome. Rina shook her head as he suggested they go into his office to talk.

'A walk, I think,' she said. 'And maybe a cup of that nice coffee.'

A stiff breeze blew across the promenade, reminding them that the summer months were almost at an end and Frantham should prepare for autumn. A few hardy souls still stripped off for a dip in the sea, and families cowered behind wind-breaks, trying to make sandcastles for their infants without being totally sandblasted.

'So,' Mac said as they leant on the railing enjoying the view, 'what can I do for you both? I take it you've moved in to Rina's?'

'For the minute,' Stan said. 'I'm not going to impose longer than I have to.'

Rina exchanged a glance with Mac but let it pass.

'And you want to talk to me because—'

'Because Rina persuaded me I owed you,' Stan said.

Mac could hear in his tone that he was now regretting the decision. He waited, knowing that Stan, like Rina, could not be rushed.

'I had this idea I could get Haines,' Stan said at last.

Mac stiffened. 'Haines?'

'Yeah, he's back. There'd been rumours so I went looking soon as I got out. I found some of his people. I don't think he's here yet, but he will be.'

'And your plan is?' Mac made an effort to keep his voice steady, his tone non-confrontational.

'Oh, I did have some idea of getting the bastard and slitting his throat, but, well, it's been suggested I leave it alone.'

'Rina suggested that? I'm glad you've—'

'No, not Rina, Stephen or Matthew or . . . well, anyway. Way I figure it, they're right. Young Karen will likely save me the bother.'

'Karen?' Mac could not keep the shock out of his voice this time.

'Apparently she's back,' Rina said.

Mac felt he might need that coffee. Or something a bit stronger.

They walked and talked and brought Mac up to speed and by the time they had reached the end of the promenade, where it curved back to join the road, Mac knew everything Stan had seen and heard. They paced slowly back towards the café, not saying a great deal.

'I need to bring Kendall in on this,' Mac said. He opened the door and led the way to his favourite seat by the window before going to the counter to place their order. It was still early in holiday terms, just after ten and in that lull between those popping in for their takeaways just before work and the pre-lunch rush of tourists and locals coming in for a snack. The little Italian café had been a feature of Frantham promenade for years, still family owned and always something of an anomaly. The first owner had been a prisoner of war in the camp across from the newly restored airfield. Like so many prisoners in rural areas, he'd ended up helping out on a local farm, fallen in love and eventually married the farmer's daughter.

Mac loved it, as had generations of Franthamites.

'So, what do we do now?' Stan said.

Rina regarded him thoughtfully. His 'plan' had sustained him all the time he had been inside. Now he was out and it was no longer a viable one; it would need replacing with something else. And soon. Stan was not a man who would be comfortable sitting around twiddling his thumbs. Rina understood how he felt, being disinclined to that course herself. He would need managing, occupying.

'Are you a good driver, Stan?'

'Am I a what?' He laughed. 'Are you planning something I should be telling Mac about?'

'No, I'm planning to get a little car, and as it's almost eight years since I last drove I could do with someone to help me get my confidence back. And while we're doing that, I thought we could take the opportunity to, shall we say, snoop a little.'

Mac returned to the table and set their coffees down, going back to collect his own. It gave Stan just enough time to change his expression into one more suitable to the circumstances.

Rina picked up her biscotti and dunked it happily. 'Smells wonderful,' she said.

* * *

Karen had booked an appointment with Messrs Colby, Price and Dicks. She had changed out of her jeans and boots and now wore a well-cut summer dress in a pale blue that emphasized her light tan and her dark hair. She carried a leather document case.

Mr Price welcomed her into his office. She had done business with his firm on and off for a couple of years now, ever since she started to earn decent money of her own and needed a means of disposing of it sensibly and in such a way as she could maintain swift access. Price and his colleagues knew she was a wealthy young woman—though they did not know about the small stashes of cash and bonds Karen had secreted up and down the country, just in case—and they knew she paid her bills promptly, and who were they to argue if she preferred to do it in cash?

Karen sat and read the document set before her and asked a few questions about the wording, which Price obligingly explained.

'It just requires your signature,' he said. 'And I can get my secretary to be witness if you'd like to attend to everything now?'

She nodded slowly and he could see that there was still something on her mind. He wondered again why such a young and obviously healthy young woman should be making out her will, and also noted that it was a somewhat unusual document. It had taken three attempts to get it to this point. There had been queries, small points of law, little anxieties. Price had discussed the matter with his senior colleague, and he was sure now that it was as unchallengeable as any document ever consigned to law could be.

'All right,' Karen said. 'I'll sign now. And I have the other documents you needed.'

He stood and held out his hand. 'I'll get them copied and verified while you have another read.'

Karen handed over a passport, birth certificate and various other documents—all expertly forged in the name of Karen Munroe—and Price skimmed through them before leaving the office to have the copies made. Karen did not bother reading through the will again, she knew the wording by heart now, carefully crafted and hopefully as secure as Price told her it would be. She glanced around the dark office. A small window seemed only to offer a view of the opposite house wall, and the light that did manage to sneak in seemed afraid to make the leap further into the room and hung around by the window. Only Price's chair was properly illuminated, and even at eleven o'clock on a sunny morning the light was on.

Price returned with his secretary and Karen signed. *K.S. Munroe.* The signature duly witnessed and her original documents returned to the leather case, Karen took her leave. She had always looked after George and this was just another aspect of that care. Whatever happened next, Karen had provided for him.

* * *

Ted Eebry didn't have a morning paper delivered so he had not seen the news about the bones. It was lunchtime when he picked up an abandoned copy of the local rag in the café where he had stopped for lunch. And there it was, filling up the front page: *Bones Found at Local Dig*.

At first, Ted assumed this was more about the skeletal remains of 2,000-year-old inhabitants. He had followed that story with great interest, discussed it at length with his daughter Stacey and her husband. Speculated about the kind of people who must have once farmed this little bit of southern England and what their lives had been like.

A quick scan of the article told him this was not the case. The bones were modern. Not fresh, but maybe a couple of decades old. Forensic tests might reveal more, but at the moment the police could not comment and the estimate of how long they may have been in the ground was subject to review. The article went on to speculate about murders and missing persons and whether or not the new airfield entrance would be ready for the official open day just over ten days from now.

Ted Eebry stared hard at the page and tried to stop his hand from shaking. His recently eaten lunch roiled in his stomach.

'Stupid,' Ted muttered to himself. 'So, so stupid.'

EIGHT

PC Andy Nevins had spent Thursday morning trawling through missing persons' reports. He didn't yet know exactly what he was supposed to be looking for, and he was getting nowhere fast. He'd decided in an arbitrary way to go back fifteen years, keep his search local and see what came up. First impressions from the forensic bods had suggested this was probably a woman's body, judging purely on the rather gracile nature of the long bone they had found, but they would not be drawn further and so Andy did not have a clue which of the several thousand reports that had emerged from his initial search he could eliminate.

Frank Baker wandered in and leaned over his shoulder.

'How's it going, boy?'

'It's not. How am I going to narrow this down, Frank? I've eliminated all the men, but I've still got two thousand and thirty-seven.'

Frank drew up a chair. 'Well, first off you get rid of those what have turned up. Most people do, usually within a week, and a good few more within the month.'

'And how do I do that?'

'Shift yourself over and let the dog see the rabbit.'

A little reluctantly, Andy surrendered the keyboard. He watched as Frank's fingers picked out letters one by one and then pressed enter. He brought up another screen and then a third, then clicked on a couple of boxes and sat back.

'What did you just do?' Andy's original search seemed to have disappeared.

'Watch and wait, boy. Watch and wait.'

Andy frowned. The screen message was telling him pretty much the same thing. How come Frank knew how to do . . . well, whatever it was he had done?

'I went on a conference thing,' Frank said, as if he had heard Andy's thoughts. 'All about searching these database whatsits. Very useful it was too. Right, let's see.'

Andy's search box had returned, but now very much slimmed down. 'What did you do?' Andy asked again.

'I took out all those what had been reported as no longer missing,' Frank said.

'What? Yes, I mean I figured that much out, but how?'

'Ah, well. I'll show you in a minute, but that's got rid of about two-thirds, I reckon. Of course, not everyone bothers to tell us when their relative comes back home, and if it's an adult and none of the social services or anyone's got involved, well there's not a lot we can do about that. What we need to do next is to use our imagination, extrapolate a bit, you might say, and see if anything stands out.'

'Extrapolate? How?' Andy felt distinctly miffed now. *He* was supposed to be the techie one in the team, not the ageing Frank. He caught sight of Frank's sly smile as he once again seemed to read Andy's thoughts. 'OK,' Andy said. 'So age and experience win this time. What do I have to do?'

'Well,' Frank continued, 'we apply a bit of psychology, I reckon. And a few statistics. The CSI tell is that the leg bone belonged to someone what had stopped growing, so we can eliminate anyone younger than, say, twenty-one. Not much sign of wear, no age-related arthritis or the like, so let's lose everyone over forty. Here, you budge back this way and work the keys and I'll tell you what to do.'

Andy scooted back across and poised his fingers over the keys while Frank told him how to manipulate the databases. He lost another third of his list.

'Now we make a few guesses. That geographical profiling mumbo-jumbo tells us people tend to dispose of bodies in familiar places, so if we temporarily remove all the hits from outside a ten-mile radius of 'ere then we've got a start point we can handle. How far back did you go?'

'Fifteen years,' Andy told him.

'Ay, well that'll do for starters. Narrow it down to between ten and fifteen years and start there. Those bones were clean, dry, and my guess is they've been around a while. I think we've gotta assume the rest of our unfortunate may have been dumped elsewhere. Big question is—'

'If they've been buried somewhere else, why move them now?'

'Right. So when we start looking for whoever did the deed, we pay attention to anything in their life what is changing now. That's a clue there, boy. Something to look out for.'

Andy nodded and stared at his now reduced hit list. It was still daunting, but if he did as Frank suggested and focused on that five-year window, something might emerge.

Frank grunted to his feet and stretched. 'I'll get you booked on the next course, shall I? Then we can both impress our technically challenged boss.'

Andy nodded eagerly and settled back to examine his list. He could hear Frank chuckling to himself as he walked away.

* * *

Mac had driven to Exeter to speak with Kendall about Stan and Haines. He found his friend and colleague about to take a lunch break and so he joined him in the canteen. Kendall commented little as Mac filled him in on Stan's new intelligence. Then it was Mac's turn to focus on his food as Kendall thought it all through.

'It fits with what we know,' he said. 'You remember that kerfuffle off the Welsh coast a couple of months back?'

Mac nodded. Friends and ex-colleagues of his had been involved in what turned out to be a complex investigation into arms deals. There'd been very little proper reporting regarding what had actually gone on and even official channels had been cagey, but so far as Mac had understood it, some government-backed agency had been mixed up in illegal dealing. 'Power vacuum?' he asked.

Kendall nodded. 'From what we can gather a couple of key players were removed from operations. One we know is dead, the other we're not so sure about but he's off the radar anyway. There have been rumours about another big player moving in to fill the void and of a possible turf war. Nothing concrete, you understand. But it's possible Haines and our old friend Vaschinsky—remember him?—are planning on pooling their resources.' He frowned.

Mac asked, 'Problems?'

'Problems in that we can't get access to the information we need. A lot of it's in a file labelled National Security and we humble policeman can't be trusted with the likes of that. As a result we're working blind. We know something big went on. We can guess that big business—of the so-called legitimate kind—and government agencies—likewise—got themselves entangled with the out and out illegal, and that whatever happened has led to a major reshuffle of the key players. We are aware of at least two organizations manoeuvring for position and our intel on the financial side is that very large sums of money are being moved around. We can only track them so far; the individual amounts are small and legal, but the number of transactions is through the roof. We didn't know about Haines being involved, not for certain, though his name came up in a report about a month ago.'

'In connection with?'

'An immigration issue. Not him, but one of his known employees. Two days later said employee turns up dead in a Birmingham canal.'

Mac frowned. 'You think Haines was responsible?'

Kendall shrugged. 'Our Mr Haines has always run legitimate businesses alongside his nefarious ones. We know he launders money through the legit side, but we've not been able to get enough evidence of how. Haines is a tax exile, lives abroad for nine months of the year and uses that boat of his like a floating home the rest of the time. His official address is a town house in Lichtenstein from which he controls his legitimate business interests, one of which is a diamond importer based in Birmingham and which this dead man, Joseph Meinen, worked for.'

'You said an immigration issue?'

'Not with Meinen. He's an EU national, living and working here quite legitimately. He'd applied to bring in a woman he claimed to be his Filipino wife. On the face of it everything seemed straightforward, but immigration did some digging and discovered this was the third potential Mrs Meinen and he'd not bothered to divorce either of the first two. They dug deeper still and twelve arrests were made. Meinen was already dead by the time they knocked on his door.'

'Haines found out?'

'Looks that way, and we both know he's not a man who likes the idea of being cut out of the profits or, for that matter, anyone that might draw unwanted attention.'

'I'd have thought a body in the canal would do that anyway.'

'Well, you would, except that it's down as a tragic accident. Meinen had been drinking heavily in one of the canal-side clubs. He left, walked along the towpath, slipped and fell and hit his head. Drowned because he'd either been knocked unconscious or was too drunk to pull himself out. The inquest approved a narrative verdict. No case to answer.'

Mac absorbed this. 'The one thing that puzzles me,' he said, 'is why should Haines turn up here now? What requires his personal attention?'

'Now that,' Kendall said, 'is the question.'

They tossed ideas back and forth for a few minutes more and then Kendall took his leave with the promise to keep Mac informed; Mac, in return, promised to keep an eye on Stan Holden. As he drove away he could not help but ask himself why he had refrained from mentioning Karen's return.

* * *

Andy returned to the dig site that afternoon, his head full of missing persons' reports and control keys used to manipulate the databases. He was glad to get back out into the fresh air.

More bones had been found, Elodie told him. She thought they might have been metacarpals and they had duly been dispatched to the lab. So that, Andy thought, meant they had a sum total of a tibia, a fragment of rib, most of one hand—the right—and a collection of random vertebrae, which begged the question of where the rest of the skeleton was hidden.

'It must have been disarticulated a long time ago,' Elodie mused as they sat on the edge of the trench.

'Why?'

'Well, Joe and I have been talking about it and the jumble of bones is really strange. I mean, think about it. If you bury a body and the soft tissue rots away and then the skeleton disarticulates where you left it, the bones would all be laid out in some kind of order. If you had to move the bones, then you'd most likely just pick up, say, the legs all in one go, then, I don't know, maybe the skull and arms together or something. We've got bits and pieces from all over the skeleton. It's just a bit strange. I mean, most people are kind of squeamish. I don't think they'd stop and sort out a confusion of bones, do you?'

A confusion of bones. Andy liked that, but he was inclined to agree. 'So,' he said, happy to continue the speculation for a while, 'what would create this confusion?'

Elodie laughed and Andy thought that if she hadn't been so obviously involved with Joe the digger driver, he'd have been summoning the nerve to ask her out himself.

'It reminds me of when the bones are dug up after burial and stored somewhere else, usually in a special box. Like a reliquary or an ossuary or something.'

'So,' Andy said slowly, 'what if the body was buried then someone had to move it later and they put all the bones into a box? Then for some reason they've got to move them again now, so they literally just pick out what comes to hand.'

'Sounds gruesome, doesn't it?'

'I've seen worse,' Andy said, then realized how that might sound. 'I mean, this isn't so bad, in the sense that it's just bones. It's not like seeing a dead person when they've just been killed. It's like . . . I don't know, easier in one way.'

'Have you seen many dead people?'

'I . . . Yes, three so far,' Andy admitted. An old lady, a teenage boy and a woman who'd committed suicide. At the time he felt he had coped well, focused on the job and on trying to impress his new boss, but he knew he was still processing the experiences.

'I must have seen dozens,' Elodie said. 'But that's kind of different, isn't it? And they've all been bones except one.'

'Except one?'

'My grandad when he died. Gran had an open coffin. Apparently it was traditional in the family or something. The strange thing was he didn't look like Grandad. He looked like someone's idea of what Grandad should have looked like.'

'Oh, if we're counting that sort of body then I suppose I've seen two more,' Andy said. 'I saw my grandad too, just after he died. I was glad I had, it was like, I don't know, confirmation. He'd been in hospital and then a hospice and we went in to see him just after he'd passed on. You know, that was the first time I understood why people say passed on, because that was exactly what it felt like. Like he'd moved. His body was there but he'd kind of left the building, you know?'

Elodie laughed. 'Yeah, I know.' She got to her feet and brushed the mud from her clothes. 'I've got to get on,' she said. 'I've got work to do.'

'So do I.' Andy scrambled upright, cursing his luck that he should meet someone so gorgeous and friendly and so easy to talk to, only to find someone else had got there first.

NINE

Ted Eebry called round to Peverill Lodge to see what Rina thought about the boxes he'd dropped off. He stayed for tea and cake, and Stan, never one to refuse either, sat with Rina and Ted and the Peters sisters as they gossiped in the kitchen.

Rina, it seemed, had decided to buy the two boxes from him. They were duly brought through from the dining room and set down on the kitchen table while Rina and Ted decided on a price. Curious, Stan picked up a bundle of papers from the closest one and flicked through while listening in to the conversation. The treasure being discussed seemed to be a mix of old playbills and programmes, a few magazines scrawled with autographs from people Stan had never heard of and a stack of photographs. There also seemed to be the odd personal letter and Stan glanced briefly at one of these. It was from a woman called Ada Barker to her sister, telling her about a booking for the summer season on Clacton pier. It was dated for March of 1953 and Stan could not help but wonder why on earth this letter could be so important that it had been kept since then.

Glancing at Rina and seeing the obvious excitement with which she and the Peters sisters viewed these innocuous contents, Stan decided he must be missing something. Always a man who travelled light, his entire possessions now resided in the little room upstairs at Peverill Lodge and amounted to the contents of one small shopping bag.

From the conversation, he gathered that this Ted Eebry was a trader in antiques and oddities. Having nothing better to do and not feeling comfortable joining in, Stan studied this stranger at the table and wondered what it was that felt wrong about him. Stan was used to reading people and situations; many times in his life his very survival had depended upon it and he'd never quite lost the habit. One thing he liked about the people at Peverill Lodge was their utter transparency. Yes, Rina was capable of guile and craftiness, but she was far too honest a soul to deceive if she didn't think it utterly necessary. And while Tim was a master of deception in his professional life, he was too utterly spaniel-like to make a success of his occasional and inconsistent attempts at generating the persona of 'man of mystery'.

Stan liked dogs. You knew where you were with them ninety per cent of the time, and Tim was just like a giant puppy, all long limbs and enthusiasm.

Rina was telling Ted about a friend of hers. Stan glanced at the leaflet she was holding which featured the photograph of a very pretty young woman in a very skimpy costume. Apparently her name was Madge Pershore and she had gone missing and everyone thought she'd been snatched and murdered. It turned out she'd just run off with a juggler from a rival act.

Everyone laughed at the story, except Stan, who realized belatedly that he should, and Ted, who chuckled in a forced and awkward kind of way as though Rina's story had touched a nerve and he was trying to hide the fact.

Stan found himself studying the man carefully, noting the strain in his eyes and the pallor of his skin, which somehow still showed beneath the redness typical of an Englishman who still did not use sun cream.

Ted Eebry, Stan thought, was a man with a secret, and it wasn't one that made him happy.

TEN

Friday evening rolled around and, after a surprisingly hot day, brought storms. Rina watched the lightning out of her bedroom window and thought about Madge Pershore and her juggler. It was so long since she'd thought about her friend, and telling Ted about her the day before had been an odd experience. From being a stranger to Rina's thoughts, Madge had become a constant companion through the day as she had recalled the things her friend had said and the fun they'd had together in those long lost days.

'I never thought you'd settle down with anyone,' Rina said as a new flash of lightning lit the rain-dark sky. 'And you had the most amazing legs.' She laughed, thinking that her own pins hadn't been so bad back then.

* * *

Ted Eebry sat in his kitchen and listened to the rain lashing the window. On the table in front of him his laptop sat open and the remaining surface had been spread with copies of the local newspaper and a couple of the national dailies. He had been tempted to buy others but knew that, creature of habit that he was, it would practically have been headline material in its own right if he had deviated further. Ted was terribly conscious of doing anything that might draw unwanted attention.

He had scoured the print pages and pored over the news sites on the Internet, but was no wiser or more informed than he'd been a couple of hours before. No more information about the bones found at the dig site was forthcoming. Not sound information anyway, just the usual round of speculation and tentative links to young women who had disappeared from the local area and turned up murdered.

'Local,' Ted scoffed. 'Since when is Liskeard local? It's two flipping counties away.' But then the report had been written by some London-based journalist, Ted thought. Like as not he saw everything west of the M25 as local to Dorset.

The local papers themselves were no more helpful. The addition of a statement from the site foreman explaining that work on unaffected parts of the site would continue as normal and that everyone was anticipating an excellent turnout on the open day was the only new element.

'I bet they are,' Ted said bitterly. Already at fever pitch, curiosity about the refurbished airfield and excitement about the fair, the music and the vintage vehicles scheduled for inclusion in the event could only be heightened by the proximity of a murder scene—which, despite all official proclamations to the contrary, was what local gossip was stating as cold hard fact. Ted snorted his disgust at such ignorant informants.

Rain lashed harder against the window and something crashed down in the garden, startling Ted from his reverie. Getting to his feet he crossed to the window and peered out through the curtain of weather at the long garden beyond. He swore softly as he realized the crash must have been the stack of plant pots he'd left beside the compost bin, brought down by the strengthening winds. One more thing to clear up in the morning.

Ted Eebry stood for a moment longer, listening to the rain and thinking how quiet the house sounded. Nothing except the ticking of the clock and the low hum of the fridge as the thermostat clicked on. Quiet and empty and . . .

Stacey was right, Ted thought. It was time to move on. The house had attracted a lot of interest since he'd put it on the market; he'd taken care of it over the years, maintained and decorated and done any little repairs himself, taking pride in his DIY skills. Time to move on.

* * *

Hill House always caught the brunt of the weather. The front and side were protected by the trees and shrubs sweeping around the drive, but the old conservatory that ran the length of the back of the house and looked out over lawn and sea always seemed to take the full force.

George stood beside the window and stared out. On one side of him was the cast-iron radiator that heated what Cheryl always referred to as the sun room. She had put the heating on tonight, bowing to the sudden shift from sun to storm, and George's left leg was much too hot while the rest of him felt chilled as he leaned close to the glass. Ursula had thrown herself into one of the tatty wicker chairs, her feet up on another and a cushion placed against the glass on which she laid her cheek. It was an indicator of her distress that her homework sat neglected on the cockled wooden table.

'I hope it stops raining by morning,' George said, needing to break the silence. 'Cheryl won't like driving in this.'

'Another reason not to go, then.'

'So, just don't go?'

'I can't not go.'

George shifted her feet and flopped down in the opposite chair. He'd reached the point in the conversation—or rather the non-conversation—when his homework actually looked like a better option. He'd not seen Ursula like this in a long time and was at a loss as to what to do, but he wanted to be 'there' for Ursula, recalling how many times she had listened to him, especially when he had first arrived at Hill House.

'OK,' he said at last, looking for another angle. 'We both know you've got to go and see your dad. If you don't go you'll feel bad, so you've got to do it.'

'If I do go I'll feel bad too,' Ursula pointed out.

'Yeah, but not *as* bad. You won't be guilting yourself for the next month.'

'True,' she admitted reluctantly.

'So we know you're going to have to go, so what can we do to make it, I don't know, not as crap as it could be? I mean, I'm coming with you—'

He broke off, not sure if that was a good thing to say or if it would sound like he was just doing it for brownie points.

'Yeah, I know, and I'm grateful, I really am. And you're right, I have to go and I have to sound all bright and pleased to see him, and I'll do all that stuff but . . .'

She chewed on her lower lip and looked determinedly out of the window. George could see the tears she was trying so hard to blink away. He knew instinctively what she was trying to say, the taboo she wanted so desperately to break but was afraid to do, and he decided the best thing was to try and do it for her.

'Sometimes I think it's easier, you know, now that she's dead. I mean it wasn't that I didn't love her and that I don't miss her, cos I did and I do. But my whole life I didn't know if she'd be OK when I came home from school. If I'd come home and she'd be . . . and then she killed herself and it was like she'd spent my whole life planning for it. I just felt so mad with her. Just so . . .' He shrugged. 'You know?'

Ursula nodded and they let the silence fall once more. George stared at the rain and knew that was kind of what Ursula had needed to hear, and how much he wished, for both of them, that it just wasn't true.

* * *

The windscreen wipers couldn't cope even on their fastest speed. Stan peered out through the waves of water, hoping nothing was coming the other way as he'd now lost all sense of where the white line should be. He and Rina had borrowed Miriam's little car and were going up to the Palisades to watch Tim perform. The idea had been that Rina should drive, but then the storm had broken and it had seemed more sensible for her first drive to be delayed until it was actually possible to see the road.

'How did you and Tim actually meet?' Stan asked.

Rina laughed. 'Oh, it was one of those strange, chance things. He knocked on my door one night looking for a place to stay and so I gave him a room. Peverill Lodge is officially a B&B after all.'

'A B&B that never has any vacancies,' Stan pointed out.

'True, but sometimes you just have to trust your instincts, don't you think? It was late, he looked so forlorn standing there. He'd been performing at a place just along the coast—I forget exactly where—and I don't think it had gone too well. He said he couldn't face the drive home and did I have a vacancy for the night.'

'And that was it?'

Rina nodded. 'More or less. He joined us for breakfast and the Peters sisters fussed over him, Matthew was flattered by some comment he'd made about the home-baked bread, and when he asked if he could stay another night while he looked for more work, I said yes.'

'And after that?' Stan caught sight of the white line once more and twitched the car back into the proper lane.

'He stayed. That was a little over five years ago and I have to say he's been my best friend ever since. Some things are just meant to be.'

Stan shook his head. 'But you knew nothing about him. You surely can't just take in strays without . . . without . . .'

'Without doing a background check? Oh, Stan, life is not that black and white. I supposed in Tim we all recognized ourselves: staying in B&Bs, working wherever we could, on the road half our lives. Sometimes life throws people into your path and you have to make fast decisions.'

'Like you did with me when I knocked on your door that night?' Stan asked her.

Rina smiled wryly. 'Well, I admit I might have hesitated had you been alone,' she told him, 'but something like that.'

They fell silent for a few minutes while Stan concentrated on peering through the now even heavier rain. 'Do you think he'll actually have an audience tonight?' he asked. 'I mean, no one will want to go out in this.'

'Oh, you'd be surprised,' Rina said. 'And I believe the hotel is fully booked anyway. The Palisades is getting quite a reputation for good food, and for good entertainment. The owners have done a lovely job restoring it.'

'Good,' Stan said. 'It's sad to see old things go to rack and ruin.'

The lights of the Palisades hotel could just be glimpsed up ahead now and Stan slowed, making sure he didn't miss the entrance to the drive. He eased the car between two pillars, illuminated by large globes, noting the old cast-iron gates fastened back on either side and the elegant sweep of drive that wound up towards the art deco building. 'Was this always a hotel?'

'I believe so. The original owner had a suite built in the west wing. The current owners live in one of the estate cottages. When it first opened all the serving staff and gardeners lived on site too. It must have been quite a place.'

Stan nodded. You could see this place from the sea, he thought, recalling his time in Haines's employ out on the luxury yacht he called home for part of the year. Was Haines out there now, watching?

He'd see bugger all in this squall, Stan thought, oddly satisfied with the little rhyme. He parked as close to the entrance as he could and fished the umbrella out from behind the seat. 'Shall we?'

'Delighted,' Rina said. 'And if this rain lets up enough, I think I'll take the wheel on the way back.'

* * *

A few miles inland the rain had eased and Karen stood in the shelter of a shop doorway watching the pub across the road. She'd followed a group of Haines's men earlier, even popped in for a drink and a sandwich, the pub offering a good selection of baguettes that reminded her of the *café-tabac* she had frequented along the Breton coastline.

Karen had found herself a comfortable corner, eaten her food and had a second drink, asked the landlord directions to Kirby St Mary and made small talk with his wife.

'Travelling over from Bristol. Got a bit lost, thought the pub looked nice so . . .'

Yes, they would remember her, but Karen didn't care. Chances were they would make no connection between the slightly ditzy young woman and what Karen planned to do—and if they did, well, Karen liked the game.

An hour ago she had left the pub, Haines's men still inside and drinking steadily. She had walked out past them, pausing in the doorway to fasten the belt on her deep red raincoat and then glanced back, knowing already that he had seen her but wanting to make certain that *he* knew *she* had recognized him. She held his gaze for a full ten seconds before turning and walking out of the door with a final wave to the landlord.

Now she waited.

From her vantage point, she could see the pub entrance and the open side gate that led into the delivery yard and through which she could just glimpse the rear door. Which exit would he choose? Karen guessed at the yard: the exit was just down a little hallway from the men's toilets so he could slip away and none of the others would notice his absence. She was in no doubt that he would come—or that he knew she would be waiting.

The final outcome, though, that was a very different thing. He would be expecting one thing and Karen was about to deliver quite another.

She didn't move when she saw him. Instead she waited and watched as he emerged through the rear door of the pub, glancing back as though to be sure that no one had observed his exit. He came out into the pub yard and lit a cigarette.

It wasn't dark yet, though it was late enough and wet enough for dusk to have coalesced here, in the back streets; she could still see him clearly enough, though, and now even the rain had abated to a light drizzle. She saw the tip of the cigarette brighten, watched him exhale, smoke drifting only for a moment in the wet air, and then he stepped out through the gate and looked around, catching sight of her in the doorway and smiling as he crossed the road.

Only when he was within feet of her did Karen move, slipping out of the doorway and facing him as he stepped up on to the pavement.

'Well, will you look at you,' Dave Jenkins said. 'All grown up.' He smiled and Karen was surprised to note that he was genuinely glad to see her.

'What are you doing here?' he asked. 'Last I heard—'

He didn't even see the knife. He had stepped closer, his smile warm. She saw his expression change as the knife slipped in between his ribs and she pushed it home. It was all over before he'd even hit the floor.

Karen retrieved the knife, slipped it into a carrier bag she'd kept in her raincoat pocket and then put that into her shoulder bag. She had blood on her coat but there was no one around to notice and the colour was disguise enough for casual glances. She turned into a side street and found her car, popped the boot and placed bag and raincoat into a black plastic sack she had left there, together with a second raincoat which, after checking her hands for blood and cleaning up with wet wipes, she slipped on. Then she drove away satisfied, and once she'd disposed of the knife and clothes, ready for hot chocolate and bed.

ELEVEN

'The way I see it,' Andy mused, 'is that whoever dumped the body had to have local knowledge. I mean, everyone round here knows about the dig, but getting the back way into the site, now you've got to know what you're about.'

'Talking to yourself?' Mac asked, sticking his head around the door to the little office.

Andy shrugged. 'At least I get a sensible discussion. What are you doing in this morning anyway? You forgotten it's a Saturday?'

'No, but then murderers never have been that respectful of weekends.'

'Murderers? You mean you've got a lead on the bones?' Andy was caught between interest and faint disappointment. This was supposed to be his case . . . sort of.

Mac shook his head. 'No, this one is a fully intact dead body. It's actually in Kendall's jurisdiction, but he wants me to take a look.'

'Oh?' Andy was on his feet. Hopeful. 'Mind if I tag along?'

'Frank says you've got enough on your plate,' Mac said.

'You mean the bones.' Andy was crestfallen.

'That, and I think he's got his heart set on some decent coffee.' Then Mac relented and stepped into Andy's cubby hole. 'You getting anywhere?' he asked.

'Not really, no. I mean we've narrowed things down a bit, but, as I was saying to myself, whoever dumped the bones has to have some local knowledge. It just seems such a strange thing to do. I mean, where's the rest?'

'Where indeed,' Mac agreed. 'Well, I'm afraid it's all yours unless you can turn up something more substantial. Cold cases are difficult even when you know who's involved. Just gather as much information as you can and then, chances are, you're going to have to draw a line under it for the moment. Unless you get lucky, of course.'

'Lucky?' Andy didn't think that was going to happen.

'If you're right and the killer, or at any rate whoever sought to conceal the death, had local knowledge, then the best thing you can do is find other sources of said local knowledge. Who'd have their ear to the ground? Who would you go to if you wanted the latest gossip?'

It was a good question, Andy thought, and one he probably knew the answer to.

'Right,' Mac said. 'I'd best be off.'

Andy nodded. Mac was right—local gossip. And though he might not be able to do anything about that today, he had a pretty good idea of what his start point might be.

* * *

Teston was a small place, with a short high street, a single shop and a pub that serviced mostly locals and was also popular with the boating community, being only a couple of miles inshore. There was only a tiny car park and that mitigated against major holiday trade, but it did catch the odd passing tourist, as the landlord was now telling Mac and DI Kendall.

'We had a few in last night. A couple meeting their friends here. Said they'd called in last season and liked the food. A young woman got herself lost, came in for directions and stopped for a bite. An old man and his niece and nephew, I think he said they were. They asked if we'd got rooms and we don't so I sent them on to The Oak, it's about three miles along the road. They had a drink and used the facilities and then left just after eight.'

'And the dead man?'

'I told you, yes, he was here with another four. Came in about half past seven and left a bit after nine. It was getting busy here by then so I can't be exact.'

'And the rest of the crowd in here were local?'

'A skittle match,' the landlord told them. 'Through in the back there.' He pointed to the area at the side of the bar, a larger, squarer room than the snug in which they were presently talking. 'The wife did the catering for it. Every two weeks we have it for the local league, so the place was heaving by nine.'

'And the dead man, you'd seen him before?' Mac confirmed.

'I told you, he and the rest, they'd been in a half-dozen times this last month or so. Never any trouble, they drank their drinks and played darts and occasionally got a bit noisy, but they quietened down if you told them.'

'And there were no arguments last night. No tension that you could see?'

The head shake was emphatic. Nothing. The evening had been peaceful and busy and he'd not seen exactly when they left.

Mac followed Kendall past the toilets and small store room and then out into the back yard. 'He must have come out this way and then crossed the road.'

'So, most likely he went to the gents, or said that's where he was going, and then came outside. That implies he didn't want the others to know, which maybe implies that he was meeting someone he didn't want them to know about.'

Kendall nodded. 'Didn't want them to know about—why?'

'Because his friends wouldn't approve? Because he was trying to hide something?'

82

'Then why come here to have a meeting with four others in tow? Why not just arrange a quiet conflab somewhere else? Somewhere private.'

'Maybe it wasn't planned. He saw someone he knew?'

Mac wandered out into the street and glanced both ways. The shop across the road was a general store, shut up after five thirty in the evening. The owners didn't live on the premises and the upper floor was apparently a holiday let, currently unoccupied, though a couple was due to arrive that afternoon. Mac had been constantly surprised since moving down here at just how many rather unlikely places were let out to holiday-makers. Though looking round he could sort of see the appeal. It was a pretty village with a pub across the road and only a couple of miles to drive to the sea, and Kendall had told him there was a garden behind the shop that residents could use.

He watched as the CSI took their final pictures and got ready to move the body. Kendall beckoned him over.

'Single stab wound,' he said. 'Whoever killed him got in close and knew what they were doing, I'd say.'

Mac crouched down beside the body. There was some-thing familiar, but he couldn't quite place it. He knew he'd seen this man before. But where?

'No ID on him?'

Kendall shook his head. 'No wallet, no phone, no keys. It looks like whoever killed him cleaned out his pockets too.'

'Maybe,' Mac said.

'Maybe?'

'I don't know,' Mac said. 'Just a feeling I've seen him somewhere. I just wonder if his friends found him and maybe they were the ones that took the wallet.'

'Any reason for thinking that?' Kendall asked.

Mac shrugged, suddenly embarrassed that he might be seen as fanciful.

Kendall led the way back into the pub. 'Not a lot more you can do,' he said. 'I just wanted you in the loop.'

Mac thanked him, his mind still nagging at the sense of familiarity, but the association just wouldn't come. 'I'd like to see the statements,' he said.

'Sure. And I'll be getting a police artist over here,' Kendall said. 'I'll send the pictures over.'

Mac nodded. 'Do that,' he said. 'I'm bloody sure I know him; I just can't place where from.'

* * *

Karen was paying what she knew would be the last visit to her solicitor. She read each document carefully before she signed, asked detailed questions she knew surprised him, and finally affixed her signature to the last page.

'And you are sure about the executor of this?' he asked. 'It's normal for us to meet with the executor of any trust, just to make sure they understand their role, you know.'

Karen fixed him with a look. 'It will all be fine,' she said. 'You just do your job. I trust Mrs Martin to do hers.'

'Right,' he said, and she could feel him quail inwardly.

'You're going away then?' he asked brightly as Karen rose to take her leave.

Karen smiled. 'You'll be relieved to know that I will be, yes,' she said. 'I've left your fee with your secretary as usual and the retainer will be transferred as arranged, just in case George or Mrs Martin should need to consult with you about anything. I expect Mrs Martin will call. She likes to be thorough.'

He nodded enthusiastically.

Karen paused in the doorway. 'I just want to ask again,' she said. 'You can see no problem with any of this? No reason that George might not get the money? No legal impediment, as you put it?'

The solicitor did his best to look affronted, but somehow she had this way of undermining his best attempts. 'You can rest assured. I'm good at my job,' he said eventually.

'I hope so,' Karen told him. 'Because I am really good at mine.'

* * *

The Brecon Wing was a secure unit, but it had a transitional area for those patients the hospital hoped would soon be well enough to be returned to the general hospital population. This, George discovered, was called Amesbury House and had a visitor's room where people could see family they'd probably had little contact with for quite some time.

Cheryl had elected to wait out in the lobby, but Ursula had begged George to go in with her and the administrator had agreed. A nurse would be on standby, sitting discreetly in the corner.

'And I'll be just outside the door,' Cheryl said again. 'If it gets too much, you just come out here and find me and we'll drive home.'

Ursula nodded. She grasped George's hand tightly and they went inside.

George had never even seen a picture of Ursula's dad, so didn't know what to expect. At least this place didn't smell, he thought, and it was actually more like a house than a hospital ward. Wooden floors were covered with rugs, and wood panels had been hung with pictures of the outside world: calm and comforting scenes of woodland and little cottages. George could almost have believed this was not a hospital, had it not been for the heavy dose of institutional green slapped carelessly over the walls of the reception.

Just why did they do that? It was a colour he couldn't stand—Rina had said it was a bit like eau de nil or something and he'd been told it was meant to be restful, but all George knew was that it was the colour of sickness, of self-harm, of his mother.

A nurse dressed in ordinary clothes sat down just inside the door and the two teenagers, hand in hand, approached a man sitting beside the fire. He was thin and drawn, but he smiled when Ursula came close.

'Hello, Dad,' she said. 'I've brought a friend. Is . . . is that OK?'

George gripped her hand tighter. He'd never felt Ursula less certain of herself.

The man got up. 'Any friend of yours . . .' he said, and tried to laugh. 'Sit down, sit down. Look, we've got tea and biscuits.'

Ursula let go of George's hand and went over to her father. She hugged him and, very hesitantly, he hugged her back, some deeply rooted remembrance of social skills kicking back in, but George could see in his face that he didn't know what to do. He began to suspect that Ursula's dad had not in fact requested this meeting. Perhaps some well meaning but, in George's view, imbecilic doctor or social worker had thought it would be good for him.

He sat down next to his friend and opposite this sad, stretched man. George recognized the fragility. He'd seen it on his mother's face so many times. Karen had tried to keep him out of the hospitals, visiting alone whenever there was anyone reliable to leave George with, and later on, when they'd had to keep moving on and his mum had been looked after most of the time just by the two of them and the fear that their mum would be hospitalized again and they'd be separated—again—because Karen wasn't considered old enough to be his carer had been nearly as great as the fear that their dad would come back . . .

Ironically, once they'd moved to Frantham their mum had been *almost* well, even able to hold down a little cleaning job provided she could go home and sleep afterwards and Karen managed everything else.

George fought those memories valiantly, but they were still there in his dreams and his quiet times and they returned with full force now.

Ursula's dad was trying to make conversation. How was school? What was Hill House like?

Ursula's responses were brief and monosyllabic and it occurred to George suddenly that even though this may be her dad, she didn't really know him. Not at all.

George took a deep breath and dived into the silence. 'Ursula's brilliant,' he said. 'She gets As all the time and the college reckons she could take ten GCSEs no problem at all and she's started to play the piano and this summer when we all played football on the back lawn Ursula played in goal. She was brilliant at that too. And I'm sorry but I don't know your name.'

Three pairs of eyes turned upon him: Ursula, her father and the nurse beside the door.

'Arthur,' Ursula's father said. 'My name is Arthur.' He smiled a little wistfully. 'It's a little old fashioned, I suppose.'

George shrugged. 'So is George. I mean, who calls their kid George these days? I used to hate it.'

'And now?' There was a spark of interest in Arthur's eyes and George fed on that. There was no pressure in this silly conversation. No having to think about the right thing to say.

'Now I don't mind,' he said. 'And I can always change it by deed poll if I want to.'

'I suppose you could.' Arthur smiled and George caught a glimpse of the man he may once have been. 'So, um, what subjects are you both taking? GCSEs—isn't that like O levels used to be? Are you old enough to be taking exams?'

'I'm fifteen this month, Dad,' Ursula reminded him.

'Oh, so you are.' The light went away as suddenly as it had arrived. 'I've missed so much of you growing up.'

Ursula looked desperately at George and he began to explain what exams they would be taking, what pieces Ursula was playing on the piano. The man listened and nodded but George could see that he'd had enough. He looked across at the nurse by the door and stood up, pulling Ursula to her feet. The nurse nodded sympathetically.

'Arthur, your visitors are going now,' she said gently. 'It's time to say goodbye.'

Arthur seemed unable even to look their way.

TWELVE

Jerry hated Sundays. He had hated Sundays as a child—no playing out in case you made a noise and disturbed the neighbours, and all day the dread of Monday slowly building. Monday and school.

Now he hated Sundays because everyone else was having a good time with their families—or at least they seemed to be doing—and Jerry was reminded of just how alone he was.

On Sundays he thought about what he might have had if he had worked things out with Louise, and life hadn't swung a sudden left turn instead. For a brief time during their engagement and subsequent short-lived marriage, he had managed to like Sundays. They had moved in together, despite her parents' opposition, and any Sunday he'd not had to work they had spent in bed, getting up only to eat. Sunday evenings had been spent in the local pub with friends, and even if he had thought about there being a Monday morning, he'd liked the job, got along with his colleagues, and the dread had faded for a while.

But that had been then. Before he'd screwed it up.

First time undercover had been a breeze. Three days. Just another body staying in a hotel. On hand in case a sting went down the wrong way. But he'd got a buzz from it, from the freedom of leaving himself behind, and when they'd looked for volunteers for a longer spell and deeper cover, he had been ready and waiting with his hand up.

Louise hadn't liked that at all. A month, this time, hanging out with a group of environmental activists, observing mostly, joining in with the odd protest and standing in line when the bulldozers arrived. He'd actually felt quite chuffed when they'd got a stay of execution for the piece of land designated as the next bypass. He'd understood what they meant about the ancient woodland the project would have trashed and he felt a quiet sense of satisfaction when the project was eventually shelved, even if the reason was more lack of funds than a bunch of hippy types tying themselves to a few old oaks.

Truthfully, Jerry had liked them and he'd felt a bit of a pang at the deceit. They had been mostly harmless and totally sincere and he felt for the first time that he was missing something in his life. Jerry had never believed in anything much, had never felt the lack before.

The next job, though, with the animal rights lot, that had been hard. He'd come home bitter and angry and in sympathy with what they were against, even while he was uneasy about their methods of protest. And Louise had given him an ultimatum: next time you say no or we are finished. And so next time he had said no and they'd got their Sundays back and he had settled into a routine he'd once loved, but which now somehow felt less real.

Louise had made him get counselling. He'd gone along to please her, but Jerry could recall how resentful he had felt. There was nothing wrong with him.

He ran his hand across the now close-cropped hair. He'd grown it down to his shoulders for a while. Added a beard, which she'd sort of liked. And he'd taken up photography in a big way. Louise had been pleased, Jerry remembered, as he sorted through the equipment in the padded backpack. Even bought him one of those khaki jackets she saw the professionals wear on the television; Jerry had laughed, but he'd put it on and after a while, as practicality outweighed his sense of the absurd, he had worn it when he went tramping off over hill and dale, as Louise would have said, searching for the perfect sunrise.

Gently, he cleaned the lens he was holding and replaced the cap. Haines had encouraged the hobby and the look; it made for excellent cover and the strange thing was, Jerry knew that if he ever found a way out of this, it would be the one thing that kept him sane and quite literally focused. He had a bit of himself that no one else could touch. Haines could make use of his skill, but that was like doing the day job. The boss makes use of you for eight hours of the day, the rest is . . .

Except it was getting harder and harder to tell where one began and the other ended. Harder to know where the old Jerry had gone and when this new Jerry had emerged, or rather sprung fully formed from somewhere inside of himself that he'd barely registered.

Others had spotted it though, seen what he really was. Didcott had seen it and been ready to exploit it. And the pressure had been applied.

Six months at most he'd been told, but he knew Louise wouldn't stand for it. He'd said no. More pressure had been applied and more than a little blackmail. The rewards he'd been promised had been . . . well, at the time they'd seemed adequate. He knew better now.

Looking back, Jerry could see how much he had been manipulated. Eventually he'd agreed. Six months, he told Louise, and I'll be able to come back regularly. He'd been naive enough to believe that at the time. Or maybe he'd just been playing her a line.

No, she had said. Go and you won't be coming back at all.

And he had, and she'd kept her word. The divorce had gone through two years after he'd come to work for Haines. Louise had seen his name blackened and his career ruined by the lies that had become his cover story, and in the end she'd not known what to believe.

Well, in the end she'd believed what the rumours said: that he was corrupt, that he was a thief, that he had beaten a man to a pulp in an interview and it had taken three other officers to pull him off.

That part had been true, Jerry acknowledged. But there'd been reasons for it. Trouble was, he'd almost forgotten what they were.

* * *

'Can't you leave your work at work?' Miriam complained mildly.

'I thought you were still asleep.'

'No fun staying in bed on your own.'

Mac smiled at her. 'There's fresh coffee in the kitchen. I heard you moving.'

He watched as she crossed to the kitchen and pressed the plunger on the cafetière. Mac was a tea drinker in the morning, but Miriam needed her coffee. She wore a blue silk robe, floor length and cinched at the waist. It had been a present from Rina, genuine art deco, the embroidery at the collar and cuffs heavy and geometric. Miriam loved it and Mac enjoyed the way it clung to her curves. He caught his breath as she pushed a heavy tress of dark hair away from her face and then came over to where he sat, mug of coffee clasped between her palms.

He had never dreamt he'd end up with someone as beautiful as Miriam.

'So, what's all this then?' she asked, settling beside him on the sofa and looking at the files and photographs laid out on the coffee table. The early light streamed in through the port-hole window and fell across her hair, illuminating the red strands mixed in with the dark. Mac moved closer, kissed her cheek, inhaling deeply.

'Maybe we should go back to bed.'

She laughed. 'And leave half your mind back here? I don't think so.'

He knew she was right. He was up and dressed now and deep in thinking mode. 'Background reading,' he said.

'These are all Haines's known associates?'

'No. Some of them are. Some of them are from other cases. I've been trying to pull together what I can about that hush-hush business a couple of months back in Wales.'

'Ah, that's a face I know. He was on the telly.'

Mac picked up the photograph. 'DI Charlie Eddison,' he said. 'Not his finest hour, but so far as we know there was no link to either Haines or Vaschinsky.'

'Hmm, and there's a photo of our friend Stan Holden. What do you think will happen to him now?'

'I don't know,' Mac admitted. 'If anyone can sort him out it's Rina. She'll have her work cut out, though. I can't see that he possesses a very saleable skill set.'

He pointed to another image. 'Santos, aka Ivram Kayne and a half-dozen other aliases. Worked for a private security firm in Iraq after the first Gulf War. We think that's where he fell in with Haines. Jerry Mason. Ex-copper, thrown off the force for corruption and assault. He'd reached DI before that and was tipped for big things. Then there's Tomas James, been with Haines, we think, for about as long as Santos, though we've got even less information about his early career than we have for Santos.'

'And has all this research helped you?'

Mac laughed. 'Not so far. I just wanted a refresher, I suppose.' He pushed everything into a pile and set it aside.

'Anything on the bones yet?'

Mac shook his head. 'We've got so little to go on,' he said. 'Poor young Andy's got stuck with the legwork. If he gets a break we can see about getting a team together. Right now Kendall tells me they've got nothing to spare.'

'It's still a murder, though,' Miriam argued.

'Well, that's the assumption. Frankly, we don't even know that.'

'So, what? Someone had a few spare bones knocking about and thought the archaeologists might like them?'

'Could be,' Mac nodded seriously. 'Truthfully, we don't have a clue. I mean we really don't have a clue. We have to see what Andy can turn up.'

'Poor Andy,' Miriam sympathized. Then, cheekily, 'I'll bet *he's* not working today.'

* * *

Ted Eebry had lunch with his daughter Stacey, son-in-law Sam and their little toddler. Ted's first grandchild, Tammy, had been a revelation to him. He had loved his own girls so much it had never occurred to him that he could feel more for any human being. But he did. Tammy was his miracle.

He played with her while Stacey got the lunch ready and Sam interfered and helped and eventually gave up all pretence of knowing what he was supposed to do and joined Ted in the living room. Sam cooked several times during the week, Stacey working three evenings in the local supermarket, but Sunday lunch was her domain and had to be done her way.

Sam flopped down into the old recliner. He'd owned it since his bachelor days and brought it with him when he and Stacey moved in together. He watched his father-in-law and little girl as they played with her tea cups and drank pretend tea, a game Tammy never seemed to tire of. He smiled. Ted was a nice old boy, Sam thought, then reminded himself that he really wasn't that old, just a bit set in his ways.

'Those boxes of stuff any good for your friend?' Sam asked.

'What? Oh yes, they were. I've got some money for you in my jacket pocket.'

'Looked like a box of old junk to me, but Stacey reckoned they'd got a value.' He laughed. 'I suppose everything has a buyer if you look long enough.'

'Rina was pleased. She knew a lot of the people on the bills. She was an actress, you know.' Ted struggled to his feet and fetched his jacket, fumbling in his pockets for the cash Rina had given him.

Sam looked surprised at the amount. 'What's that? Fifty? For that load of old junk?'

Ted shrugged. 'Rina liked it,' he said. 'Reckon she'll have a lot of fun going through it and remembering old friends. We were selling her a dose of nostalgia, I suppose.'

Sam laughed. 'Well you'd better give that to the boss. I told her whatever the stuff fetched could go into the holiday fund.' He sounded faintly regretful now the boxes of junk had fetched more than he had anticipated. He bent down to scoop his little girl into his arms. 'You got a cup of tea for Daddy?'

Tammy giggled and Ted watched, a heavy weight wrapped around his heart.

* * *

Andy had managed to get back to his mother's home for a few hours, immersing himself once more in the sibling-heavy squabbling, noise and laughter that characterized her house.

Andy, oldest of the brood, had moved out almost as soon as he'd started police training, and though his bedsit wasn't anything to shout about, he was loving the independence— *and* the quiet *and* getting off the Jubilee Estate where he'd grown up and where being a police officer wasn't the typical career choice. He missed his family though; his mother had raised all five of them alone when their father had died. The Big C, as his Aunt Bec still called it, taking his dad only six months after the diagnosis, though Andy realized now he'd been ill for a lot longer than that but just hadn't wanted to confront the fact. Andy, then eleven, had done all he could to help the rest of them through it, taking over the cooking when his mum had to get a job with more hours. Susie, the youngest, had only been two.

He'd not said that he was coming to Sunday dinner, but he knew that didn't matter. They'd be glad to see him and his mum and Aunt Bec—a fixture on a Sunday since the last of her own brood had left home—would be eager for any gossip he might feel able to impart. Andy was always careful about what he told them, but boy were they good at wheedling. Frank Baker always reckoned Andy's mum and aunt should have advertised their services as interrogators.

Lunch over, Andy helped his mum with the washing up, the only way he could guarantee getting her alone for a bit. Or almost alone. Aunt Bec installed herself at the kitchen table with a fresh pot of tea and lit a cigarette.

'So,' Aunt Bec wanted to know, 'why aren't you on that murder investigation? The one out near the pub at Teston.'

'Because the CID at Exeter got that one. I'm looking after the bones at the dig site.'

Bec didn't look impressed, but his mother was interested. 'Any news on that, is there?'

'No,' Andy admitted. 'I'm trawling missing persons, but it's a job and a half. You'd never reckon so many folk just drop off the planet.'

''Ow far you goin' back?' Bec asked, and Andy knew he'd hooked her. He celebrated silently and played it cagey; best to be a bit conspiratorial with Bec and his mum.

'Oh, we've narrowed it down far as we can, but . . .'

'There was that woman end of Newell Street. Ran off and left her kids. Hilda someone. Must be thirty years ago now.'

'Too far back,' Andy said.

'And old Mrs Took. Though I always reckoned her son just put her in a home.'

'Too old,' Andy said. 'If she was old enough to be put in a home.'

'You think it's a young woman then?' his mother asked.

'Youngish. I mean, best guess is between twenty-five and fifty. There's not enough bones for anyone to be really sure.'

Bec snorted. 'Bit of a spread you got there, ain't it? I thought these 'ere CSI could tell to the year what age a corpse was.'

'It's not a corpse,' his mother defended. 'It's just bones. It's not the complete skeleton, then?' she asked, picking up the implication from what Andy had said.

Andy shook his head. 'Just a sort of random selection.' His mother and aunt exchanged a look. 'This is confidential stuff, you know,' he reminded them, and comforted himself with the thought that anyone who actually read the local papers would have been able to figure that out for themselves anyway, so it was *almost* public domain, though as neither his mother nor Aunt Bec read anything more exacting than the odd female magazine, he had to admit they'd never have found out themselves.

'So.' His mother dried her hands and took a seat opposite her sister. 'What are you looking for? What sort of missing woman?'

Andy wiped and stacked another plate. 'That's the thing,' he said. 'The bones were clean and dry and we reckon they'd been stored somewhere else. Best guess is the woman died not more than twenty years ago, but it could be as recently as five. And it was somewhere they hadn't been disturbed by wild animals or anything. No teeth marks on them or 'owt like that. And—' he took a deep breath—'boss reckons they were local and whoever dumped them was local and knew the place well enough to get there at night without falling in a ditch or getting caught on the cameras up at the site.'

These had, in fact, been Andy's own conclusions, but he knew his mother would take Mac's view much more seriously.

Bec snorted again. 'We all know where the cameras are,' she said. 'Up on that damned great pole.'

This was true, Andy thought. They'd been set high and made deliberately obvious in the hope this might persuade the kids on the Jubilee Estate that it wasn't worth their bother to thieve from the site.

'So. A local girl, then.'

Andy noticed that his mother had automatically gone for the younger age estimate and diminished it still further. It was funny, he reflected, how the young and the very old garnered more sympathy when they were dead or lost. The middle-aged seemed to make less of a ripple in the public consciousness.

She and Bec exchanged another meaningful glance.

Andy waited.

'You'll need your notebook then,' Bec told him. 'And a pen. There's paper and pen on the side near the telephone if you've forgotten yours.' The thought of Andy without the tools of his trade made her laugh.

'Best get the paper and pen anyway,' his mother said. 'Those silly little books they give you, what can you get in them?'

Obediently, Andy went through to the hall and took the note pad from beside the telephone, then braced himself for a long afternoon.

* * *

Lunchtime at the Martin household was interrupted by the sound of the letterbox rattling. Rina would have assumed a delivery of junk mail and ignored it, but she happened to be about to go through to the kitchen to get more gravy, so she glanced at the mat on her way through.

The package that lay there was definitely not junk mail.

Gravy boat in hand, she bent to pick the stuffed brown envelope from the floor. Just her name on the envelope, but in handwriting she recognized. Rina opened the front door, but she knew the young woman who had posted the envelope would already be gone.

Karen, Rina thought. Now what?

Unwilling to interrupt the Sunday ritual and knowing if she was much longer getting back to the table a search party would be sent out, she opened the door to her private sitting room at the front of the house—her one real sanctuary—and slipped the package on to the table just inside. She went on into the kitchen, her mind in turmoil. Karen meant trouble. Karen always meant trouble.

It was another hour before Rina managed to escape, and even then she knew it would be wondered at. Tim, recognizing something odd in her manner, followed her as only Tim was entitled to.

'What is it, Rina?'

'I'm not sure. It seems to be some kind of legal document. Well, several legal documents.'

Tim read over her shoulder. 'A trust fund,' he said. 'And a will. What's Karen playing at?'

'I think she's still looking after George,' Rina said. 'And she seems to have made me her executor. Whatever she's up to, my guess is either she's going to leave for good afterwards, or she thinks this time her luck might finally run out.'

* * *

Ted returned home late in the afternoon. There was a message on his phone from the estate agent asking him to ring back to arrange another viewing, this one from a couple who wanted a second look. She sounded enthusiastic and hopeful, despite evidently having to work on a Sunday; probably calculating her commission already, Ted thought.

He stood in the hall and listened to the slight sounds—the fridge, the ticking of the clock, the creaks and groans that every house made and that after all these years he was so terribly familiar with—and he knew that Stacey was right. It was long past time to move on. To leave this place.

Every day brought new memories and new guilt. It wasn't that he'd ever expected the guilt to pass, but he had never envisaged how, with the passing years, the memories would pile upon memories and the might-have-beens beckon ever more painfully.

He had never removed her pictures, not even in those later years when the children had stopped asking when mummy would be coming home. It had been five whole rounds of Christmases and birthdays and anniversaries before he had even summoned up the nerve to remove her clothes from the wardrobe and her cosmetics and jewellery from the dressing table drawers. In the weeks after the event—that was the way he always thought of it—he had moved into the spare room, unable to bear the thought of sleeping in that bed, looking at those things that did not belong to him and now did not belong to her.

In the end it had been Stacey who had forced the issue. Tired of sharing a room with her younger sister, she had asked him straight out.

'Can't I move into your old room? You never use it now.'

At first he had been stunned. Shocked by what he thought was the unfeeling attitude of a teenage girl, willing to wipe out all trace of her mother. Gail had backed her up. She had been five when it happened, she was ten now, and wanted to have friends on sleepovers without having to share her space with a big sister now into music and pop stars and boys.

'You never sleep there anymore. It's a sad room. I'll help Stacey if you like. You don't have to do any of it and then I can paint my walls green and have a bunk bed with a spare bed underneath, like I showed you in the catalogue.'

'But . . .' he had objected. He'd been about to say, what if she comes back, even though he knew that was never going to happen.

'She's gone, Dad,' Stacey said. 'She's gone. She doesn't care about any of us anymore, so why should we care about her? You should find someone else.'

He had wanted to tell them that it wasn't true, that their mother had cared, that she probably still would had she been around, but he just couldn't bring himself to trot out the platitudes they must have heard hundreds of times—from him, from their friends, from their relations. And so, though he had dug in his heels and argued about it for a day or two, the deed was done. The girls packed their mother's clothes into boxes and bags and sorted through the jewellery and photographs and silky scarves that she had loved so much, and chatted about what they could remember of her and what they just thought they could recall.

Stacey had kept a few odds and ends. He had found photographs he had forgotten even existed, and some strings of bright beads decorated his older daughter's dressing table mirror for a week or so, before they got in her way and were consigned once more to the drawer. Occasionally he would catch sight of something their mother had owned: a ring, a scarf, a pair of red leather gloves. And he knew they still talked about her, speculated, wondered, though never in his hearing and far less now than they had done in those early days.

Life settled and continued and eleven years had passed since Stacey took possession of what had been their room. When she left home, Gail moved her stuff in, but only briefly. She left for university and came back only when she felt compelled. She still called him once or twice a week, sent him texts when she remembered, and occasionally he'd open his email to find a picture or two of his youngest child.

He knew she censored them, sending only those images which showed her in the most suitable light, but he didn't mind. He, against all the odds and all of the gossip, had done a good job with his girls and he was proud. Of them and of himself.

But the memories . . . Well, unlike daughters, they continued in residence, year after year, day after day, a solid and ineffable presence, settling more solidly and more ineffably as the years passed and the house emptied and the quiet settled.

Ted sighed and closed his eyes. 'I'm sorry,' he told his dead wife, love of his life and companion of his soul even now that she was dead and gone and lost to him. 'I am so sorry, lovely. I would never have hurt you. Never.'

THIRTEEN

Monday morning brought a positive identification for the murdered man: David Jenkins, aged thirty-eight. 'No actual criminal record,' Kendall told Mac, 'but he's been a person of interest in a number of investigations. Until now, he's always managed not to be there at the crucial moment.'

'Looks like his luck ran out on Friday night. Known associates?'

'Ah, now that's where it gets interesting. He was listed as crew aboard *The Spirit of Unity* when they had that little run-in with the coastguard a couple of years back. Haines's yacht.'

'So he probably knew Parker, George and Karen's father.' Mac thought about it. Was that where he recognized the man from? Had he seen him when he first came to Frantham eighteen months ago? 'Can you send a picture over?'

'Should be waiting in your inbox already alongside his rap sheet. PM says a single stab wound, double-edged knife—the pathologist is a bit of a whizz at these things and he reckons something like a Fairburn Sykes blade, much beloved of our special forces boys. I don't suppose—'

'Count Stan Holden out,' Mac told him. 'I'm afraid he has an alibi. He was with Rina Martin on Friday night, watching Tim Brandon perform along with another hundred odd people.'

'Right.' Kendall sounded disappointed. 'Well, I'll send over what we have so far, might be worth talking to Holden anyway, likely he'd have known the dead man. And the police artist has pictures of his friends. I've sent them over as well, but you know how these things are. Show them to him anyway, he might just recognize someone.'

Mac agreed, thinking he should talk to George too. Funny how, when listing possible suspects, Mac couldn't help but put Karen Parker at the top.

He'd just got off the phone when Andy came through and told him Rina had called. She wanted a word whenever he could manage it. The timing seemed just too appropriate.

'Give her a ring back, will you, Andy? Tell her I'm on my way now.'

On the short walk to Peverill Lodge, Mac replayed the events that had led to his association with George and Karen Parker. He'd not been in Frantham long and a break-in at an old lady's house had led to his first encounter with Rina, and later his meeting George and Karen.

Life had been complicated for the children: violent father and depressive mother, Karen trying to substitute for both. And then the father had come back on the scene and everything had come to a head. Mac knew all too well that Karen was as capable of violence as her father had been, the difference being that Parker had been a common or garden thug; with Karen, well, her skills had been honed to something resembling high art.

And this meant it was time for a rethink. He'd wanted to believe that Karen had come back just to see her brother, though he'd always known she must have some other reason. Had she come back to deal with this Dave Jenkins? Did she also plan to deal with her father's one-time boss, as Stan Holden had suggested?

He really ought to tell Kendall she was here. Not doing so in the first place hadn't made a lot of sense; not doing so now was purely irresponsible.

Unusually, Rina was alone at Peverill Lodge, apart from Stan, who hovered uncertainly in the kitchen doorway as she let Mac in.

'Where is everyone?' Mac asked as he followed her through to the back of the house and took his usual place at the scrubbed table.

'Tim's taken the ladies out for a while; they wanted to do some shopping so, bless his heart, he's playing taxi driver and referee.'

'Referee?'

'They don't think I know but apparently they are off buying my birthday presents. You know how it would be if I liked one present more than the other.'

Mac laughed. 'I can imagine.' He made a mental note to remind Miriam about Rina's birthday. She was far better at choosing gifts than he was. 'And the twins?'

'The boys have gone off to the Marina to have lunch.'

'Oh, of course, it's Monday,' Mac said. 'I'd forgotten that. So what did you want to see me about?'

'I didn't expect you to come straight over?' Rina made a question of the observation.

Mac smiled. 'No,' he said. 'But as it happens I need a word with Stan.' He took the pictures Kendall had sent over from his jacket pocket and set them on the table. 'David Jenkins,' he said. 'I'm guessing you knew him?'

Stan nodded warily. 'He works for Haines. What about him?'

'He was stabbed to death on Friday night,' Mac said. 'Oh, I know you didn't do it, but what I would like an opinion on is the likelihood that Karen Parker did.'

'Karen?' Rina sounded shocked.

Stan picked up the photograph and studied it carefully. 'He was thick with Parker,' he said. 'I think they'd known each other a long time.'

'So it's likely he'd have known the family?'

Stan shrugged, then nodded. 'Maybe. I didn't like Parker, had as little to do with him as I could get away with, but I've got a feeling Jenkins was the one that recommended him to Haines.'

'And could you speculate on why Karen might want him dead?'

Stan shook his head slowly. 'I can speculate,' he said, 'but no more accurately than you could. Jenkins was as much of a thug as Parker, but he was smarter, faster, better at getting away with it. Haines used Parker when all he wanted was a bit of muscle. Jenkins was better at persuasion, if you see what I mean.' He cast an uncomfortable glance in Rina's direction.

Mac nodded. 'So,' he asked Rina, 'what did you need me for?'

'Karen,' Rina said. She got up and fetched a brown envelope from the dresser. 'I found this on my doormat yesterday. I could do with some advice.'

Mac read through the documents Karen had left and drew the same conclusions Rina had done. 'What's she playing at?' he wondered. 'Rina, I think you need more than my advice on this. I think you need to talk to the solicitor who drew these papers up.'

'Oh, I've already made an appointment,' she said. 'He seemed to be expecting my call, but I thought you ought to be kept in the loop, as they say.'

Stan replaced the pictures on the table. 'She never had direct dealings with Haines, did she?'

'Not as far as we know.'

'But he was complicit in what her dad planned to do. He knew what Parker had in mind and he approved. He said family should be loyal and Karen deserved all she got.'

'But there's no direct link to Haines other than her father's employment.'

'No,' Stan said thoughtfully. 'But I heard things about her and about a chap called Vaschinsky. I think he and Haines were thick.'

Mac nodded. 'We met once,' he said. 'I know he wasn't happy with Karen. He tried to have her killed. She escaped.'

'But the price is still out there. Vashinsky's still prepared to pay. Haines would kill just for that.'

'You think he's threatened Karen?'

Stan shrugged. 'I wouldn't know. All I do know is Haines gets around to everything in time. I'll be on his list somewhere, probably Karen is too. Maybe she plans to get in first.'

'Then why put him on his guard by killing one of his men?' Rina argued. 'No. I think this is personal. She was after this Jenkins for her own reasons.'

'And now she's done that she'll bugger off?' Stan laughed. 'You're both kidding yourselves if you think that. I know people like Karen Parker. They don't back off, not until they've completed the mission.'

'Mission?'

Stan shrugged. 'Call it what you like. She's got something in mind, something big. I figured from the start it would be about dealing with Haines. And before you object on the ground that Haines had no direct dealings with her, stop thinking like a logical, normal person because Karen won't be. If she wants him dead then she'll find a reason.'

Rina was momentarily taken aback but Mac nodded. What Stan said felt right. It felt like Karen.

FOURTEEN

Ted Eebry hadn't gone to work. He'd been due to bid on a couple of mixed lots at the local auction house, but somehow he could not bring himself to go. Once there he'd have felt obliged to talk to people and Ted wasn't sure he was up to that particular task.

Instead, he'd driven into Honiton and found a stationer's he'd not used before and bought himself a will form, visited a convenience store for a bottle of cheap gin, and then come back and dug around in the medicine box for the strong painkillers left over from the time he'd dislocated his shoulder and the sleeping pills prescribed for Stacey after she'd got so stressed during her exams.

The labels on the pill bottles were faded and he didn't bother to look at the dates on them. He'd been meaning to take the unused medicine back to the pharmacy for years, just like those adverts in the doctor's said you should, but it had never seemed to get to the top of his list; instead, the tablets in their childproof containers had slid further and further down into the depths of the biscuit tin he used as a first aid box.

Ted had come home and locked the doors, lined up the gin and pills and the folded form on the kitchen table and spent the past half hour looking at them and wondering what to do next. He'd heard such horror stories about people who had not taken enough pills and had woken up with half their organs wrecked, or people who had taken too much at once and then just made themselves sick. He vaguely remembered reading somewhere that you should take the pills with milk, something to line your stomach, but he wasn't sure if that was a real memory or something that had got itself conflated with his dad's advice about going out in a boat.

Ted, unlike his dad, had always been a lousy sailor.

He wished he had the courage to get his computer out and Google the question, but that just seemed so inappropriate, and Ted always had this odd feeling that if you searched for something like that it would be found out—somehow people would know.

Taking a deep breath, Ted did what he always did when faced with a dilemma. He got up and put the kettle on.

From across the room Ted surveyed the pills, alcohol and unwritten will. Leaning against the kitchen counter he folded his arms across his chest and thought through his options one more time. He could give himself up to the police, but after all this time he'd have a hard job getting anyone to believe Kath's death had just been an accident. I mean, why cover something up if it hadn't been deliberate? Or he could go on as normal and hope no one put two and two together and worked out they added up to Ted.

Or he could . . . leave.

The kettle boiled and Ted made tea and took the pot back to the table, setting it down between the gin and the pills. Somehow, the old brown pot diminished the potency of both. Ted took a mug from the rack and poured a large measure of gin, sniffed it suspiciously and wondered why on earth he had bought a spirit he didn't even like. His logic had been exactly based on that. He much preferred a nice drop of whisky, but the idea of using a single malt or even a good blend for such a purpose somehow appalled him. Scotch was for celebration, not for doing yourself in. He took a sip, grimaced. It always tasted far too perfumed for his liking and he'd not even remembered to buy any tonic.

'Oh, Christ,' Ted said. 'This is just stupid. Who do you think you're kidding, Ted Eebry?'

Embarrassed now, he poured the gin back into the bottle, spilling half of it as he did so. Then he cleared the pills and booze from the table and stuffed them into the cupboard under the sink, hiding everything behind the bottles of bleach and wash powder.

He didn't want to die. Kath hadn't wanted to die. Killing himself wouldn't make Kath any less dead or anything else less complicated; it would just leave a mess behind for his girls to deal with. Ted could not bear the thought of causing them such distress or inconvenience.

His hand trembled as he poured the tea in the mug and cupped it between his hands, quite forgetting that he should have added milk. He could still smell the gin.

'I'm sorry, Kath,' he said. 'I'm so sorry, my lovely. I never meant to do anyone any harm, least of all you.'

FIFTEEN

Mac met George and Ursula out of college and walked with them back into town. Ursula seemed unusually subdued, he thought, and George was both worried and pleased to see him.

'What's up?' George asked.

'Does anything have to be up?'

'Yes, if you're waiting for us to get out of school. If this was a social call then we'd all be at Rina's or somewhere.'

Mac laughed. 'I suppose we would,' he agreed. 'George, did your parents ever mention a man called Dave Jenkins?'

'He was a right creep,' George said. 'Dad used to bring him home and Mum would get in a panic every time he did.'

'She was afraid of him?'

George thought about it and then shook his head. 'Not exactly. I mean I think she was, but, I mean, she was scared of everything. It's like she was half scared of him and half, I dunno, sort of . . . she'd always wear something nice when he came round, make sure she'd got a bit of make-up on, that sort of thing.'

'So you think she flirted with him? And how did your dad react to that?'

George found that one much harder to answer. He looked away, Mac noted, and a slight flush rose to his freckled cheeks. George was always pale—a classic redhead with almost translucent skin, and a tendency to blush when he was under stress.

'George . . .' Mac prompted gently.

Ursula shot him a look that told him his pressure was not welcome.

George shook his head. 'I dunno.'

'Oh, for God's sake,' Ursula exploded. 'You want him to say it, Mac? George's dad pimped his mum. He wanted her to get all dolled up for this Jenkins person. It was just another of the despicable things he did.'

George's blush deepened but he did not contradict Ursula, and Mac suddenly felt very awkward and very stupid. But there was another question he just had to ask. 'And Karen?'

'Sometimes you can be as thick as . . . what do you think?'

Mac was taken aback.

'He would have done,' George said quietly. 'But Karen knew what was going on. Soon as she could she made us leave and she kept us moving. She kept us safe. She tried to anyway.'

'I'm sorry, George,' Mac said. 'I'd not hurt you for the world, you know that.'

'Isn't that the kind of lie adults always tell?' Ursula marched on ahead and George and Mac both stopped and stared at her.

'George, is she OK?'

George shrugged. 'She went to see her dad at the weekend.'

'And that's bad?' He was doing it again, Mac thought. Being stupid. 'Sorry,' he said. 'I guess it must have been.'

They walked on. Ursula had slowed down now, seemingly torn between her fury at Mac and not wanting to turn up at the bus stop alone. She'd get teased about falling out with her 'boyfriend' and that would be just too much to bear right now. She didn't look at either of them when they caught up with her, but she didn't pull away when George took her hand, just bowed her head lower and Mac realized she was crying.

'Ursula, if there's anything I can do . . .'

She mumbled what might have been a thank you. George managed a half-smile. Mac watched them walk on, feeling like he'd caused all of their troubles and wanting to make things right, though he'd no idea what that might involve.

Maybe he should talk to Rina.

Suddenly tired, Mac turned and walked back to his car.

SIXTEEN

Mac had caught Kendall on the way into work on Tuesday and perched on his desk drinking coffee while his colleague made phone calls and shuffled paper around.

'Anything more on Haines?' he asked when Kendall finally laid the phone to rest.

'Not a lot, but it looks like he and Vaschinsky might both have fingers in the same pie. It all leads back to that business a couple of months ago.'

Mac nodded. 'I had a chat with an ex-colleague last night. It started when a journalist called Jamie Dale broke a story, or rather she tried to.'

'I saw the reports. I'm still hazy on the details, but from what I can gather she implicated several politicians, some very big corporations and a handful of high-up civil servants.' Kendall grinned. 'Seems every time you open a newspaper there's another dozen queuing up to resign and at the same time swearing on their honour they did not take bribes and they certainly didn't sell weapons to proscribed governments.' He gestured his disgust.

'From what I can gather someone released her material to the media after she'd died.'

Mac nodded.

'Well, I'm sorry for her, but to be brutal about it, I don't see that she made a bloody bit of difference. The deals are still being done, it's just new people doing the buying, new intermediaries setting up the deals, and a few new faces doing the selling, but you can bet your pension nothing else has changed.'

Mac laughed. 'What pension?'

'Quite. But seriously, Mac, it looks increasingly like Haines and Vaschinsky are after a slice of the action while there's still something left to carve up. Our intel is that they've pooled resources.'

'Not natural bedfellows, I wouldn't have thought.' Vaschinsky had links to the Russian Mafia, whereas Haines had always been something of a lone wolf.

'I'm sure they'll manage if there's a big enough bed,' Kendall said. 'One more thing, though, and I'm giving you the heads up on this much against the wishes of my bosses. We've got someone on the inside. With Haines. Looks like what little we do know is down to him.'

Mac frowned. 'Not where I'd want to be,' he said.

'Me neither, but it looks like he's our best hope of taking Haines down.'

* * *

Andy's mother called him at work, an event rare enough to cause the young man to panic. 'What's wrong? Are the kids alright?'

The kids—like he was the parent and not the elder brother.

'Oh, we're all fine, love. I'm calling about the, what do you call them, leads you were looking for.'

'Leads?' Alarm bells began to ring. Andy smiled sheepishly at Frank Baker who was watching him with an amused look on his round face. He retreated into the back office, to the extent that the phone cable would allow. He could hear Frank chuckling to himself. 'Mum, I—'

'We've been asking round, discreetly, like. Now don't you worry, no one mentioned you, we just got to talking with the girls, you know, about strange things that happen and people what go missing and we've come up with a bit of a list, me and Aunty Bec. You got a pen?'

'You already gave me a list, Mum. I—'

'I know we did, but this is like a refined list. A proper thought through one. You caught us on the hop the other day. Now are you ready with that pen?'

Andy sighed, but obediently grabbed pen and paper. He was writing for some time.

Frank Baker watched as he came back through to the front office and replaced the phone. Andy had a notebook in his hand and an expression on his face some way between embarrassment and excitement.

'Frank, do you know any of these people?'

'Let's take a deco. The Franks girl, yes I remember her, we always reckoned she just got sick of her parents, but might be worth following that up. Ditto Miss Emmory, though in that case it was the older sister who probably made her leave, a real old battleaxe. Kath Eebry . . . well, who knows? He was distraught, I remember that much, but we got nowhere with the case. Trouble is, Andy, when a woman that age goes missing and there's no evidence of foul play, I think there's always that idea she don't want to be found. Same with the Franks girl.'

'You think these are worth a look, though?'

Sergeant Baker nodded. 'You've got to start somewhere and your mam's right, these were both local women and the cases were a bit off. Give them a go, I say, and if you draw a blank, pick some more names off that list. As things stand we've got nothing better.'

* * *

Rina had decided to take the plunge and had walked with Stan up to the De Barr garage to look at cars. The road out of Frantham wound its way up the hill and on to the cliff top. It was one of Rina's favourite walks, with wonderful views almost all the way up. Stan spent a lot of it glancing out to sea.

'Memories?' Rina asked him.

'Some.' He laughed. 'One or two dramatic ones. I suppose I keep expecting to see *The Spirit of Unity* out there.'

'Is that likely? Won't he want to keep a low profile?'

'I doubt it. More likely he'll want me and anyone else to know he's around and can strike any time he wants to. Like I said, I'm just not at the top of his list yet.'

They paused a few hundred yards from the garage at a spot where the view was particularly spectacular. The De Barr hotel was now just visible round on Druston Head and Frantham bay laid out in all its glory below them. It wasn't a large bay, Rina thought, but she loved it, relished the way the cliffs reached out to embrace the little town that had become her cherished home.

'What do you *want* to do with your life?' she asked abruptly.

Stan laughed. 'Direct as ever.'

'I suppose. But it seems to me that you've drifted a bit. That you've not actually made any conscious decisions for a long time.'

Stan thought about it and wondered if he was offended by the suggestion; found that he wasn't. 'Not since I left the army,' he agreed. 'I suppose even before that. I mean, once you join up your future is directed for you in some respects. You've got a path to follow.'

'And now?'

'Now I feel like I've stepped off this cliff top and not even tried to stop myself from falling,' Stan said. 'So I can't answer your question, Rina, because the truth is I haven't got a clue.'

She nodded as though that's what she had expected. He wondered if he'd disappointed her and then decided not. Rina wasn't a woman who indulged in making judgements;

she just did things, sorted stuff. He wondered if she ever got tired of being the facilitator and decided that he was not yet enough of a confidante for her to tell him even if she did. That was the sort of thing she'd confess to Tim or maybe to Mac.

'So,' he said, 'what car are you after then?'

She smiled. 'I rather think it will be a case of what De Barrs have got,' she said. 'So get your negotiating head on, we're going to get ourselves a deal.'

SEVENTEEN

Andy had spent Wednesday morning driving around the countryside close to Frantham and offending people. Or at least that's the way it felt. Those he hadn't offended he knew he had upset, and so far it had gained him nothing.

There had been Mr and Mrs Franks, whose daughter had gone missing ten years ago at the age of twenty-two. They had been cautiously welcoming when he'd knocked on their door.

Andy had sat in their kitchen and drunk tea and asked if they had heard from their daughter since her disappearance.

Mrs Franks had pursed her lips and shaken her head. Mr Franks had taken to staring out through the window at the very tidy garden.

'You've heard about the bones we found at the dig?' Andy asked cautiously. 'So we're reviewing old cases?' He'd made a question of this last, hoping they would take the hint and respond with one of their own.

They didn't. Andy was left to plough on without help. 'So we're, as I say, revisiting relevant missing persons' reports and looking to eliminate any that . . . well, that might have been in contact since.' He paused, looked from one to the other. Where was Frank Baker when you needed him?

'Those are not her bones,' Mrs Franks said eventually.

'You've heard from her then?' Andy realized he sounded too eager, but surely it was a good thing if they knew where she was and it was one he could cross off his list.

Instead there was just a silence, one that grew increasingly uncomfortable as the seconds ticked on.

'Do you know where she is?' Andy asked at last.

Mrs Franks shook her head. The lips were tightly pursed again.

'No more would we want to,' Mr Franks said. 'She made her choice and she must live with it.'

'I don't understand,' Andy said.

'Went off with some foreigner,' Mr Franks said. 'We told her if she stuck with him she needn't bother coming home again.'

'You reported her missing,' Andy said.

'And so she is and so far as I'm concerned she can stay that way.' Mr Franks got up abruptly and pointed at the door. 'So if that's what you've come for I think you should go now.'

'So you know she's alright?' Andy persisted. 'You reported her missing.'

'That was before we knew,' Mrs Franks said. 'Then she sent us a letter. Told us where she'd gone and that she was with him. Said she hoped we could forgive her.'

'It would have been helpful,' Andy said, 'if you'd let the police know. Your May is still listed as a missing person.'

'And have the whole world know what she'd done?' Mr Franks demanded.

Andy left shortly after, leaving the Franks bristling with indignation.

Then Mrs Emmory and her seven cats. Her sister had left home without a word eighteen years before, never a word since, and what did Andy think he was doing dragging all that up again?

Having half suffocated on the smell of cats and litter trays during his brief stay, Andy could not help but sympathize at the sister's departure.

Then two dead ends, people having moved on and the new residents ignorant of any tragedy relating to their homes until the moment Andy knocked on their front doors. And the three heartbreaking encounters with parents who believed he may have finally brought news when he really had none. He had drunk tea, left his card, spoken words of sympathy and wished fervently that he had been able to get hold of a family liaison officer to make these calls with him. Frantham, being such an outpost, had no such personnel attached, and it would have meant trying to co-opt someone from Exeter. Andy hadn't thought there'd be a cat in hell's chance of that happening on short notice.

By two o clock he felt wrung out, had a bladder bursting with too much tea, and thoughts tumbling and moiling in an overfull brain.

The bladder sending too insistent a message, Andy pulled over at a farm gate and discreetly relieved himself behind his car. Afterwards, he paused for a moment, leaning on the gate and enjoying the view across the rolling field and out to sea. He loved this place, had been born and cherished here, and he could think of nowhere better. He thought of the Franks and their daughter and her foreigner, their refusal to reconcile, and compared them to the Reeds, who he'd just left, still grieving for their teenage daughter and who would have given anything to know that she'd just run away with someone. He thought of his younger sister, Lizzy, and what their mam would think if Liz chose someone she might not approve of. Lizzy was sixteen and currently their mother didn't really like any of the assorted boys vying for her attention. But that, Andy knew, was just parental anxiety. Once Lizzy chose someone their mam's only concern would be that her child was happy and that her man was good to her.

Andy knew that he or his siblings would have to do something really drastic to earn such radical disapproval, and even then he suspected their mam would go all out to protect them, even if that meant doing something drastic like breaking the law. Not, Andy admitted, that his mum had a lot of time for what might be called conventional morality as represented by the local police. He was well aware of how much his own career choice bewildered and amused her. He also knew that she was proud of him, and that mattered a great deal.

Reluctantly, Andy got into his car and drove to the last person on his list. He knew Ted Eebry quite well, having been in the same school class as his youngest daughter and part of the same loose group of friends. He'd fancied Gail something rotten when they'd both been fifteen or so, but she'd always gone for the better looking—and older—boys. Then she'd gone off to uni and he'd gone to do his police training, though they were still friends on Facebook.

He pulled up in front of Ted's house, wondering if he'd be in at this point in the afternoon. Ted had always kept rather odd hours. He rang the bell and waited, noting the For Sale sign nailed to the front gate post. So Ted was moving on? Andy found it hard to imagine him living anywhere else. This had always been the Eebrys' house, one of a small group built in the seventies by some developer or other who, so his mum said, had planned to create a full estate on the outskirts of Frantham, only to fall foul of the local planners or not have enough money or something like that. In the end there'd been a half-dozen homes built around a green crescent, about half a mile from the Jubilee Estate where Andy had grown up; a hundred miles away in terms of class and affluence.

'He's not home,' someone shouted from across the road. 'Went out about an hour ago.'

Andy turned and wandered over to where another familiar from his teenage years smiled across at him. 'How's it going, Andy?'

'Fine, thanks, Mr Jones. How's Bee?'

'Oh, still engaged, still as empty headed.' He laughed. 'You looking for Ted?'

'It'll keep,' Andy said. 'Any idea when he'll be back?'

'Sorry, no. He can't have gone far. He didn't take the car.'

'Right.' So, should he wait? Andy wondered. In the end he decided he'd come back another time. He'd had enough for one day and wanted to talk to someone who wasn't going to be offended by his questions or overwhelmed by the grief they caused, and he wasn't sure which camp Ted would fall into.

Getting back into his car, Andy cast his mind back to when Kath Eebry up and left. He and the Eebry girls had still been in primary school . . . No, that was wrong, Stacey had already gone up, hadn't she? He recalled Kath Eebry as being a happy, friendly woman who always kept chocolate bars in the kitchen drawer, but he could bring little else to mind apart from the distress her daughters had suffered when she had gone away. They'd stopped coming to school for a while and he sort of remembered that they'd gone off somewhere and come back after the summer holidays.

Such a major event, Andy thought. In their lives and so, by proxy, in his. The more he pressed the memories, the more he could recall of the local gossip and speculation and one odd thought he'd had a couple of years later when he'd lost his own father in very different circumstances. He'd thought, at least I know where my dad's gone. It would have been terrible if, one day, he'd just not been there and he'd always had to wonder if and when he might be coming back.

EIGHTEEN

'How's it going?' Mac asked later that afternoon, popping his head into Andy's cubby hole.

'It's not,' Andy told him forlornly.

'You want to tell me about it?'

'It's just all so overwhelming. I'm asking all these questions and some people don't want me to rake everything up again and others, well, you can see they're just waiting for news, like their entire life has been put on hold, just waiting for me or someone to come and give them answers.'

Mac sat down in the other chair. 'It's tough,' he said. 'You're doing a good job, Andy. None of this is easy and you should really have more backup on this, not be handling it on your own.'

Andy sighed. 'Sorry,' he said. 'It all got a bit much today. And I'm not getting anywhere, that's the frustrating thing.'

Mac listened while Andy filled him in on the day, about the Franks and the rest and his remembrance of Kath Eebry.

'You going back to talk to him?' Mac asked. 'Feel like some company?'

Andy nodded. 'That would be welcome,' he admitted.

'Tomorrow morning, then. I'll pop along with you and then I think we ought to pay a visit to the dig site, I've not had a chance to see the crime scene yet.'

Andy nodded. 'Anything on that David Jenkins?'

'Not yet. Stan Holden has seen the police artist and taken a look through our pictures of Haines's known associates. He's given us some additional details, but . . . Kendall's keeping me informed.'

'Does that feel frustrating?' Andy wondered. 'I mean, kind of being on the outside.'

'A little,' Mac told him. 'But not as much as you might think.'

* * *

Ted Eebry had been out to fetch the evening papers when Andy had called. He'd taken a walk to the newsagent for the local papers and one of the nationals and then nipped into the little convenience store and added others, popping them guiltily into his shopping bag. He'd never found time to read more than one paper a day, often not that, and here he was scouring half a dozen some days, searching for any little scrap of news.

Of course, the few bones found at an archaeological dig had been soundly beaten into second place by the news of some man's death out at Teston. The man's picture appeared in the papers this time. His name was David Jenkins. Ted glanced at his picture and at the artist's impressions of the men who had been with him, and then moved on, searching assiduously for any glimmer of news about *his* bones.

There was nothing new. Nothing.

He'd driven past the site every day. Seen the police cordon and, before this David Jenkins got himself killed, the little encampment of journalists and even a television news crew down at the road end. Even they had gone now, chased off after richer pickings, and Ted supposed he should be relieved. This might all blow over.

Then he looked again at the friendly little note that Andy Nevins had left, asking Ted to give him a ring when he had a minute, and he knew it wasn't over yet, however much he might wish it to be.

* * *

Haines was also reading the newspapers. They lay scattered across the impressive desk in his hotel suite, together with the report from the pathologist and the latest faxes and emails pertaining to the police investigation. Haines liked to be well informed; he paid good money to be kept up to date. So far, though, he knew nothing that he hadn't known yesterday.

'Stan Holden talked at length to DI MacGregor,' Tomas said. 'We can guess what he'll have told him.'

'Perhaps. Our Mr Holden always had an agenda of his own. He may well be selective in what he decides to impart. I don't believe he has a great love of authority in any form, least of all the law.'

Tomas gestured impatiently. 'I still say we bring him in and find out.'

'And I agree. Where we disagree, Tomas, is in the timing. I need to think about this. It may be that we can make some use of our Mr Holden.'

'Use? How?'

'With regard to Parker's daughter,' Haines said.

'And I've already told you. We can take care of that.'

'Oh, maybe you could, Tomas, but it would amuse me to watch Stan Holden have a go at solving that particular problem. It would amuse me and it would save you the trouble, shall we say.'

'What trouble? She's a kid. A little girl.'

'Who most probably killed Jenkins, don't forget that.'

'Jenkins was thinking of getting his end away.' Jerry Mason laughed. 'Jenkins was always—'

'Probably,' Haines said, cutting him off. 'We all know Jenkins has history with Parker and his family and, frankly, if this was a simple matter of revenge, I might well let it go. The girl showed skill and nerve and, remember, Tomas, she may be young but she's thorough and about as conscienceless as you are. Parker was trash, Jenkins not much above that. I allowed Parker to take his shot at his daughter; the way I figured it, I owed him the chance to get even. She tried to kill him. It was only fair he got the opportunity to return the compliment. Karen won that round and I've got to admit to a sneaking sympathy with her attitude towards Jenkins. So, as I said, had it been possible, I might just have let matters lie. However . . .'

'However?'

'I have friends who would like to see Karen Parker retired.'

Tomas laughed. 'Vaschinsky.'

'Among others. But Vaschinsky is, shall we say, a better payer than most. So, I thought we could let our friend Stan have first go, and then, when he fails, Tomas, you can take your best shot. Look,' he added, raising his voice for the first time, 'Karen Parker is just a sideshow, an amusement. Yes, I'd like her out of the picture, and if that's a profitable course then it's worth looking at. What she isn't worth is time and effort we don't have to expend. Don't lose sight of why we're here, of the bigger picture.'

There was a brief silence and then, as it became clear that their audience was over, Tomas and Jerry Mason wandered out of the hotel suite and back towards their own rooms, adjoining those of their boss.

'See the whole picture,' Tomas mimicked. 'Don't lose sight of the main game. Maybe we'd keep a better eye on the game if he actually bothered to tell us what it was.'

Jerry laughed. 'Like that will ever happen,' he said. 'International man of mystery is our Haines.' He frowned. 'What the hell do you reckon is going on?'

Tomas shrugged. 'So long as he keeps paying me I'll keep not asking daft questions.' he said.

* * *

Jerry Mason sat alone in his room, television on, drink in hand, but he wasn't watching the screen and he'd barely touched his drink. He was a worried man. Six months, his handlers had told him. Just six months. That had been close on three years ago and here he was still playing paid thug to

Haines's master criminal, using his connections to keep his current boss fed with the intelligence that was like meat and bread to him. Sending information back the other way.

It occurred to him that he was no longer sure which side he was on, which persona now dominated. Who he'd take note of if one side tried to set him against the other. It had been three weeks since he'd been able to make proper contact with his handler, if you didn't count that one brief phone call. Three weeks since that anchor point had been reinforced. Right now he felt like a participant in some bizarre S&M role play who had forgotten his safe word and wasn't convinced the other participants would care even if he managed to remember it.

And there was more. He had followed Dave Jenkins to the toilets at the back of the pub a few minutes after he had made the excuse and left the table. He too had recognized Karen Parker that night and had guessed something was going on when she had left and exchanged that look with Jenkins.

Jerry had been the one to raise the alarm, come back to the table and tell them Jenkins was not in the toilets, but by that time, of course, he was dead and Karen gone. Jerry Mason had made sure of that and he was still not certain why. He had followed Jenkins out into the yard, watched from the shadow of the wall as he had crossed the road to where Karen had been standing. Watched as she had stuck the knife between his ribs and then walked away. Watched until she had turned the corner and then disappeared from view; only then had he returned to the table and expressed surprise that Jenkins was still not back.

'I could have stopped her.' He took a sip of his drink. The ice had melted and the spirit was dilute and insipid. 'Could have, didn't.'

So what side of the law had that put him on? True, he didn't want to blow his cover—he was under no illusion as to what would happen to him should he do that—but he could, quite legitimately, have shouted a warning to Jenkins, have tackled Karen himself or drawn the attention of the others to the fact that she was there. So why hadn't he?

He had sanctioned Karen's execution of David Jenkins. Perhaps even aided it.

He sipped at his drink again and mentally added that to the list of other ambiguities, other times when he had well and truly crossed the line, and he acknowledged that it was not the fact of crossing that line that troubled him. Undercover, you didn't always have a choice of what rules to break. It was the fact that he no longer cared.

NINETEEN

The meeting on Thursday afternoon with his probation officer, Tina Marsh, had not gone particularly well, but he had survived it, Stan thought. It seemed to have centred on the question of him getting a job, and as Tim Brandon had already spoken to the owners of the Palisades and they had agreed to give Stan a trial, he at least had something positive to offer in response.

The job didn't really have a title. They needed someone to do general maintenance and be an all-round dogsbody. It would only be part-time and it was subject to everyone getting on and them being reassured that Stan was not about to rob guests or murder anyone, but it was a start.

'I went up and had a chat with the owners,' Stan reassured Tina Marsh. 'Look, this is their phone number, they said to phone if you'd got questions.'

Tina Marsh pursed her lips and looked doubtful. 'And how did that go? The conversation with the owners.'

'Well,' Stan said. Able to answer that with some confidence. 'Rina told them about me—'

'Rina. Mrs Martin.'

'Yes.'

The pursed lips thinned even further. 'I'm not sure—'

'Look, she's a friend of DI MacGregor, ask him for a character reference if you like. Fact is, she's helping me out with a place to stay and helping me to find work. I really don't see what you could have a beef with?'

Tina Marsh shuffled her papers and set them aside in a Manila file. 'I have your interests at heart here, nothing more.'

'And I appreciate that.'

'Then you'll keep me informed. Same time next week?'

Stan nodded and made his escape, trying to figure out if Tina Marsh was actually trying to help or if her default setting was just disbelief in any kind of positive humanity.

His preoccupation was probably the cause of his lack of alertness, and that momentary absence of attention was enough. He had turned down the side road at the corner of the building when it happened. Someone grabbed him from behind. Another someone hit him hard and Stan sagged, stunned. He struggled, but dazed and confused could not break free. Another blow took even that consciousness away. The world went black and Stan was bundled, helpless, into a waiting car.

TWENTY

In the end it was without Mac, who'd been called away for a meeting with Kendall, that Andy finally caught up with Ted Eebry. Having not heard from him, Andy had taken a chance on knocking at his door on the Thursday afternoon. Ted had opened it and looked momentarily shocked, a not unusual reaction in Andy's experience.

'Hi, Ted, how you doing? It's been a long time. How are the girls?'

Ted seemed to relax. 'It has,' he said. 'A very long time, our Andy. You'd best come in.'

He stood aside and Andy stepped into the once-familiar space. It had changed little from what he remembered, apart from a few extra photographs on the wall of the hallway and an absence of school bags and coats on the hooks just inside the door.

'I'm making a brew,' Ted told him. 'Mind if we go through to the kitchen?'

''Course I don't. How are you keeping? I saw the For Sale board. I never reckoned on you moving?'

'Oh, there's a time for everything as our Stacey keeps telling me. I've put in an offer on a little bungalow just down the road from her and the babby. I've been doing a lot of work

130

with her Sam just lately and it all makes sense, you know. Closer to family and all that. You see much of your mum?'

Andy sat down at the kitchen table. The same table, he noted, same chairs. Even the same canisters for tea and coffee, though the black writing had now worn so badly it was hard to make out which was which. 'Oh, she's fine,' he said. 'Kids are growing like weeds and she's doing more hours at the pub now and a bit of an early morning cleaning job.'

Ted poured boiling water on to the tea. 'She always did work hard,' he agreed. 'So what can I do for you? Neighbours said you called the other day and I found your note, I've just not got around to—'

'Oh, that's all right. Tell the truth, Ted, it feels weird to be coming round here all official.'

'I expect it does. Last time you sat at that there table you were stuffing your face with beans on toast.'

Andy laughed. 'Probably,' he agreed.

'You were always hungry.'

Ted set the pot and mugs on the table and sat down. 'So what can I do for you?' he said.

Andy, who'd had his opening gambit all prepared, was suddenly at a loss. This was Ted Eebry, a man he'd known for most of his life, who . . . Andy put such thoughts aside and tried to get his professional head back on.

'It's about those bones we found up at the dig site,' he said. 'Ted, I know it might seem totally irrelevant, but we're opening up a lot of cold cases, missing persons and that sort of thing. It's just routine, you see, and—'

'And you think those bones might be our Kathy?'

'Well . . .' Andy wasn't sure what to say. 'We're looking at a lot of possibilities. I just wanted to give you the heads up, you know, see if you'd had any more thoughts? I know it's a long time ago . . .' He trailed off and Ted poured the tea.

'Look, son, I know you've got to look at these things, but that's not my Kath buried up there.' He set the pot back on the table and fixed Andy with a stare. 'I hope you don't plan on bothering our Stacey with any of this?'

Andy shook his head vehemently. 'Oh no. Nothing like that. This is just routine, part of a list, you know?'

Ted glared at him a moment longer and then nodded and pushed the sugar bowl in Andy's direction. 'It hit the girls hard,' he said, 'Kath going like that. They thought it was something they'd done, you know. But I told them, sometimes people just have to do what they have to do. Kath obviously felt she'd . . . well, if I'd known what she'd felt I may have been able to do something about it, but you get my drift. Andy, lad, she met some fella and went off with him. That's all there is to it. Sad but really simple.'

'You know that for certain?'

'No, I don't know it for certain, but it's a reasonable assumption, isn't it? I knew she was seeing someone. Never did know who, but when she went off you can bet it was with him, whoever he was.'

Andy added sugar to his tea and stirred. 'I always had the impression you had no idea what had happened to her.'

Ted shrugged and stirred his own tea, even though he'd added no sugar. Rina did that too, Andy thought. 'At the time I thought it was better if the girls didn't know. I thought it might be harder for them to think their mother had chosen some man over them. Maybe I was wrong. In fact, almost certainly I was wrong, but you know how it is, Andy. You do your best, do what seems to be the right thing at the time.'

'I suppose,' Andy said. 'It must be a very hard thing to deal with.'

They fell silent for a moment and then Ted asked, 'So no clues left with these bones then? No clothing or anything like that?'

'No,' Andy said. 'Nothing useful like that. Just a collection of bones dumped in the trench. It's sad, you know?'

Ted nodded, but he looked puzzled.

'This was a person who belonged somewhere,' Andy continued. 'Chances are, like Kath they were reported missing, only whoever this was didn't just go off somewhere. They were taken away and killed and then, years later, dug back up again and dumped like rubbish. Even if we do find out who it is, the family won't be able to give them a proper burial. It's just a few bones.'

Ted stopped stirring his tea and stared at Andy. The spoon fell from between his fingers and clattered against the edge of the mug. It was Andy's turn to look puzzled and then contrite. 'Sorry,' he said. 'I shouldn't have said that. It's just been a long old week and I don't think I've even inched things forward.'

Ted smiled a little shakily. 'We all have weeks like that, lad,' he sympathized. 'Drink your tea and take a breather, you'll feel better for it.' He laughed, suddenly. 'You know what I always thought about me and your mum?'

'No, what?'

'That we both did a bloody good job of raising our kids. One-parent families we might have been, but you and yours and me and mine, we did all right, didn't we?'

Andy nodded, not quite sure what he should say to that. 'Yeah,' he said. 'I think we're all turning out OK.'

Ten minutes or so later, Andy left Ted Eebry's house and drove away. Something was chafing at the back of his brain, but he couldn't put his finger on it. Whatever it was, he knew it would be rubbing him sore before the day was over. Best leave things alone when they feel like that, his mum had always told him. Let your mind sort it out and like as not you'll wake up with the answer at three in the morning.

Andy could attest to the truth of that.

In part what was bothering him was Ted's sudden certainty that his wife had gone off with a lover. Andy recalled Kath well, and the pictures he had seen of her reinforced the knowledge that Kath Eebry had been a very pretty woman. He could remember the gossip when she had disappeared, some of the more catty reflections being that Ted had, from the start, been the wrong man for her. Short and slightly tubby even as a young man, he'd not been the best looking or the richest or the most dynamic, but Andy could remember that he'd always been kind; he'd assumed that Kath had valued that fact. And she had loved the girls. Loved them passionately, Andy was sure of that. Would she really have just up and left?

He needed to talk to one of her friends from back then, find out what they thought and if anyone else knew she'd been having an affair.

Feeling that he needed wiser minds than his to work this one out, he tried to do as his mother had suggested and put the problem to the back of his mind, sat it in a corner and left it to nag.

'Something's not right here, Ted Eebry,' Andy said, and cursed the fact that it would most likely be him that had to sort it out.

* * *

After Andy had left, Ted had continued to sit at his kitchen table, staring into space. He felt as though the walls were closing in on him and he kept telling himself that there was no one else to blame.

Andy's words had cut so deep, filled him with even more guilt. He had never meant . . .

Ted Eebry buried his face in his hands and wept.

TWENTY-ONE

Stan awoke slowly and tried to take stock. His head thumped, beneath his cheek was something that felt like carpet, and he could hear men's voices in what sounded like the far distance but as consciousness returned he realized was actually very close by. Too muzzy-headed to make out the words, Stan focused on how the rest of his body felt and found it was in no better shape than his head. He hurt. Everywhere. Like someone had been using his unconscious self as a punch bag.

Dimly he recalled coming to in the car and hitting out at someone who then hit back. He knew he'd ended up lying in the footwell of the car, fending off fists and feet until he'd passed out again, and he hadn't even had the satisfaction of landing anything in return.

The voices were swimming back into aural focus and he recognized two of them: Santos and Haines. The third he thought might be Jerry Mason. Dimly he recalled seeing Mason's face in the car.

One of them had noticed that he'd woken up because he heard footsteps and felt hands tight on his arms as he was hauled to his feet.

Stan's head lolled back and he gasped for breath, realizing for the first time that the additional pain was the all-too-familiar one that went with busted ribs. He fought to bring his head upright as someone pushed him backward into a chair, but he felt like a bad case of whiplash. He could taste blood.

Haines's face came into almost focus as Stan stared at him.

'My, my, Mr Holden. You do look a mess. You should know when not to fight.'

'What do you want?' The words came out slurred. The taste of blood freshened, iron metallic now instead of just stale and coppery.

'A trade,' Haines said. 'A debt paid, you might say.'

'And if I say no?'

'Then I let Santos and Jerry finish what they started. I doubt it will take long. Another kick to the ribs, maybe a coup de grâce to the head. I'm told you know what it's like to have a punctured lung and I'm also told it's not an experience anyone wants twice.'

It was not, Stan agreed. He spat, trying to get the blood out of his mouth, hoping it would hit Haines, but he didn't have the strength for it. Blood and saliva dribbled down his chin and dripped on to his hands. Haines frowned. Santos laughed.

'Wipe his face,' Haines said.

Jerry Mason trapped Stan's hands beneath his own and scrubbed at his chin with a tissue.

'Now,' Haines said. 'Do we have a deal?'

Stan tried to laugh. He managed a hoarse croak. 'You've not told me what you want,' he said.

'We've established, I think, that you'd like to live. I'd have thought anything after that was a bonus.' Haines leaned a little closer. 'I want the Parker girl dealt with,' he said.

'Then deal with her,' Stan said thickly.

'No, I think it better that you do. Call it outsourcing. Deal with Karen Parker and I might just leave you alone.'

'Like that's going to happen.'

'No, I can't promise that it will. But a chance is better than none, isn't it? Deal with Karen Parker and, as I say, I might just leave you alone.'

Stan decided to try another tack. 'What is she to you?'

'She killed one of my people. I don't like others doing what it should only be my right to do. You know how I feel about people interfering.'

'So she did for Dave Jenkins, did she?' Stan's attempt at a laugh sounded more convincing this time. 'Good for her.'

Next minute he was gasping for breath again as Santos's fist buried itself in his gut. He retched. More blood and then dry, rasping gasps as he doubled up in pain. Mason hauled him up, crashing him back into the chair.

'You are a stupid man, Stan Holden. A very stupid man.' Haines sighed. 'Oh well, since you won't do this for yourself, perhaps you'll exercise a little of that famous altruism of yours. Karen Parker was not an only child, was she? Ah, I see that's got your attention. George, isn't it? Nice looking boy, if you like red hair.'

'She'll kill you,' Stan gasped out.

'Not if you get to her first,' Haines said.

TWENTY-TWO

It was still not fully dark when Stan was dumped out of the car on to a grass verge. He lay still, listening to the receding sound of the engine as the car sped away and almost gave in to the impulse to just lie there, wherever *there* was, and go to sleep.

His ribs were beyond painful. Every breath sent stabs of agony through his chest and his head felt like it was twice its proper size and being held together by an ever tightening steel band. Slowly, he turned from his side, where he had landed, on to his hands and knees and promptly collapsed again as the arms proved unequal to the task. He tried again, relying more on the legs this time, and eventually, awkwardly, struggled to his feet and looked around.

Where the hell was this?

He stood at the side of a narrow country road, grass verges and a mix of stone wall and hedge separating the road from fields. He couldn't see much beyond the hedge—a combination of dusk and rising land made sure of that—though he could make out the last vestiges of sunset off to his right. So that was west, then, or approximately west. Not that knowing his compass points helped much, Stan thought; he might set off in one direction looking for help and find it was much quicker to get to if he'd chosen the other way. He'd have to make a guess.

He felt in his pockets, knowing even before he did that they'd be empty. Haines had taken everything: phone, money, even the assortment of till receipts and bus tickets he'd tucked away. It was pure spite on Haines's part, depriving him of anything that might be useful. He supposed he ought to be grateful the bastard hadn't taken his clothes and shoes.

Santos had driven him out here. Jerry Mason and one of the newcomers Stan didn't know had accompanied him, Jerry in the back, gun pressed to Stan's ribs all the way, just in case he got any smart ideas.

Stan's fingers moved up to his shirt pocket. He never kept anything in there so it was just a vain hope. He was surprised, therefore, to find a little slip of paper that looked as though it had been torn from the bottom of a newspaper page.

Curious, Stan took it out and looked at it. He could just make out a name and what looked like a phone number in the gloom, but recognized neither.

'What the hell is that?'

Stan sighed. Too worn out and in too much pain for puzzles, he slipped it back into his pocket and stepped out into the road. Left or right? He turned right, not from any sense of conviction but because the last streaks of sunset somehow cheered him. Praying that some kind of civilization would be close by, Stan limped on.

* * *

Back in his little bedsit, Andy logged on to his computer while he ate dinner, pecking at his food with a fork in one hand and at the computer keyboard with a finger of the other.

He was still thinking about his missing people and about Ted Eebry; still discomforted by the nag at the back of his mind.

It wasn't unusual for Gail Eebry to be on chat at this time and he noticed she was on tonight. It was his usual habit to say hi and exchange a few comments, so he knew it would be a bit odd if he didn't do that now. So he did, and in the course of their conversation said he'd seen her dad that afternoon.

'Oh? He OK?'

'Fine, yeah.'

Andy's finger hesitated over the next sentence. What to say? *'I had a cup of tea with him. Not been round yours in years.'*

'Lol, not much change. Got it up for sale.'

'Yeah, I saw. Didn't think he ever would.'

'No, Stacey nagged him. Don't think it was his idea.'

He knew she'd ask and he was dreading the next question.

'Why go to see him?'

'Oh, bit awkward. Working through cold cases.'

There was a palpable delay before she began typing again.

'You mean Mum?'

Again, what to say? *'Just routine. Checking loads of old cases.'*

'Why?'

'They found some bones at the dig site near the aerodrome. Stacey tell you about it?'

'No.'

This time they both hesitated and Andy finally typed: *'Sorry to talk about it this way.'*

'Yeah. Look, I'd better get going, you know.'

'Sure. OK. See you next time you come back?'

The pause was so long this time he thought she'd gone, and then she typed back, *'We never stopped wondering, you know? Do you think it's her?'*

Andy groaned. Boy, what a question. *'We don't know anything yet. I'm working through a very long list.'*

'But Mum is on it. You really think it might be?'

God, Andy thought, he'd not expected this sort of reaction. And surely this wasn't the sort of thing you should chat about on a social network site? '*Gail, I really don't know. I'm sorry. Look, your dad said today he thought she'd gone off with someone, so . . .*'

'*He said that? Don't be daft, Andy. Dad never thought that. Why would he say that?*'

Andy didn't know. '*Look, I've got to go,*' he typed, taking what he knew was a cowardly way out. '*I'll give you a ring if I find out anything else, OK.*'

This time there really was no response forthcoming. He logged out and sat staring at the computer screen. His food was cold, and he pushed it away, not wanting to eat now. Not wanting this kind of responsibility. It just wasn't fair.

* * *

When Stan had not returned home for dinner, no one had been unduly worried. They knew his appointment was not until three and Rina's view of officialdom was that they never kept to any sort of timetable. Her new purchase from De Barr's garage had arrived that afternoon and been oohed and aahhed over by the other inhabitants of Peverill Lodge. She'd even taken then for a spin around town, the little blue hatchback slightly cramped for four and the driver, but gaining general approval all the same. Tim had admired from a distance, standing on the pavement and waiting for them to get back. Rina realized he was actually quite anxious about her first solo flight and truly relieved when they returned safely.

'Oh, it's not that I don't think you can do it,' he said when she challenged him about it. 'Just that I remember you saying how much you hated driving.'

'I did,' she admitted. 'But I think this little car and I might well become friends. She's happy and easy going, so I think I'll be just fine.'

When Stan still hadn't returned before Tim left for work, the Montmorencys expressed some concern. 'He could have called and let us know,' Matthew said.

'I don't think he's used to having anyone to care,' Rina reminded him. 'I don't imagine he's used to having anyone worry.'

By eleven, even Rina was anxious. She'd tried to call twice to Stan's mobile phone, and twice someone had hung up. The third time a mechanical voice said the number was unavailable. She was on the verge of calling Mac, debating the matter only because it was already so late, when the house phone rang. It was Stan.

* * *

Santos was in high spirits when they got back to the hotel and reported in to Haines. His high spirits were undiminished by their boss's apparent lack of interest in what they'd done with Stan. It was typical of Haines, Jerry thought. He appeared to lose interest once something was dealt with. Appeared being the operative word.

Santos and the others went down to the bar. Jerry, knowing it was out of order not to, joined them and sat watching as Santos re-enacted the defeat of Stan Holden.

'Personal for you, was it?'

'Bastard always thought he was too good for this. Anyway, he shot Coran.'

'You hated Coran.'

'And? Coran was one of us. Stan never was. Some people never make the grade. They make the right noises, but they never really make it.'

He turned and looked pointedly at Jerry. Jerry raised his glass in mock salute and Tomas laughed, the rest joining in.

He saw the barman look their way and then busy himself with the ice bucket when he caught Jerry's eye. What did the staff here make of them all? he wondered. Haines might just have passed for a businessman, but what kind of businessman travelled with an entourage of eight armed thugs? Not that the staff knew about the guns, Jerry supposed, but one look at his associates was enough for most people to take

142

avoiding action, and it was noticeable that only a half-dozen others now remained in the bar and they were packed into a corner at the furthest end.

'Enjoy yourself today?' Santos asked, drawing close to Jerry in a quiet moment.

'Not as much as you did,' Jerry said. 'I don't have quite your enthusiasm.'

Santos laughed. 'Like I said—' his voice was low so only Jerry caught the words—'not everybody makes the grade, do they?'

TWENTY-THREE

It had taken Stan three hours to cover two miles and he had staggered into the yard in front of the Fisherman's Rest just on closing time.

'He says he got hit by a car,' the landlord told Rina as he met her at the door. 'Hit and run, that's what he said. That he was walking and someone hit him in their car. I wanted to call the police and an ambulance but he wouldn't have any of it, said he had a sister nearby and you'd come and get him.'

A sister, Rina thought. Somehow she didn't think anyone would believe that she and Stan were related. He was sitting beside the bar in an easy chair that had been dragged over from the snug. He looked half dead, she thought. Bruises and blood all over his face and his clothes and skin grey as ash.

'I should have called the ambulance,' the landlord fretted.

Rina laid a hand on his arm. 'I'll take him home,' she said. 'Thank you so much for looking after him. Stupid bugger, I keep telling him about these late night walks, but he won't listen.'

'And the police? If it was a hit and run—'

'Look,' Rina said. 'Call a friend of ours, will you? Detective Inspector MacGregor. Tell him what's happened and that I've taken Stan home, ask him to meet us there. If you get a pen I'll give you his number.'

The landlord went off to find a pen and paper and Rina bent down to examine Stan. 'Lord, but you are a mess. I'd have called an ambulance and tied you to the chair if you'd argued.'

Stan managed a smile. 'You're not going to, though, are you?'

'No,' she admitted. 'But I'm going to live to regret that, I think. Can you stand up?'

The landlord came back and Rina gave him the number for Mac's mobile.

'Right, let's get you into the car.'

It took several minutes to get Stan installed in the passenger seat and covered with the blanket Rina had brought with her. The landlord came out and told her DI MacGregor would meet them back home. He seemed a little happier now that the forces of law and order had been called upon.

'So,' Rina asked as they drove away, 'what actually happened to you?'

'Haines,' Stan said.

'Haines? In that case my next question is: why aren't you dead?'

'Hell, thanks.' Stan grimaced. 'I'm not so sure I'm not.'

'It's supposed to be painless,' Rina reminded him. 'So, tell me. What's going on, Stan? What have you been up to?'

Receiving no response, she glanced sideways. Stan had closed his eyes and exhaustion had won. Rina slowed down and took a better look, just to satisfy herself that he was in fact still breathing.

'Don't you dare die in my new car, Stan Holden. You turn my car into a crime scene and I'm not going to forgive you. Just remember that.'

Haines, she thought. She reached out and locked the doors. Lord, Rina Martin, when trouble comes knocking at your door you really are going to have to learn to tell it to bugger off.

* * *

Matthew and Stephen had helped Stan to get undressed and had washed away the worst of the blood before helping him into bed on the sofa. It was very obvious he wouldn't be able to make it up the stairs. The Peters sisters fussed around, finding the smoothest sheets and the softest blankets, and Eliza produced butterfly sutures Rina had no idea they possessed from a first aid box she had no idea existed, and eased together the cuts on Stan's face.

She saw Rina looking at the box. 'We decided we should be prepared,' she said. 'There's been a lot of drama since Mac came to Frantham, so we thought we should put some proper survival kits together.'

Rina decided that now was not a good time to ask more, especially when Eliza went on to produce some very powerful-looking painkillers and insisted on examining Stan's ribs.

He accepted the painkillers and reassured her about the ribs. Broken, but nothing he'd not endured before. He could still breathe; he just needed to rest.

Gently, Mac ushered everyone away and then drew up a chair next to the couch. 'You should see a doctor. There might be internal bleeding.'

'Might be, but I don't think so. I'm not dead yet. If Santos had damaged my liver I'd have bled out by now. If he'd punctured a lung I'd still be lying on the roadside and I doubt I'd still be breathing. I just need to rest. Pass me my shirt, will you? Look in the pocket.'

Mac did as he asked. Puzzled, he looked at the name and number.

'Someone put that into my pocket. Mean anything to you?'

'I'm not sure.' Mac frowned. 'Why would anyone do that?'

Stan shook his head and closed his eyes.

'So, tell me,' Mac said. 'What happened and what did Haines want you for?'

'He wants me to get rid of Karen for him,' Stan said. 'And when I told him to spin on it he threatened her brother, George. I told him he must be soft in the head but he meant it, said I'd be free and clear if I did what he wanted; when I said no he threatened the boy.'

Stan's head lolled sideways and when Mac called his name he didn't respond. Whatever Eliza had given him, it was powerful stuff.

'What do we do?' Rina asked as she walked Mac through to the hall and he told her what Stan had said. 'And does that number mean anything?'

Mac hesitated. 'I'm going to talk to Kendall,' he said. 'Don't worry, we'll take care of George.'

'And the number?'

'I'm not sure yet, Rina. Kendall said they'd got someone on the inside of Haines's operation. It's just possible—'

'That it might be from him?'

TWENTY-FOUR

Mac returned to visit Stan early the following morning, Friday. He was sitting at the breakfast table, but it was pretty clear that even that was an effort. They helped him into the living room and back on to the sofa, and Mac went through the events of the previous day.

'What I don't get,' he said at last, 'is why Haines would want you to go after Karen. He has the resources to take care of her himself.'

'I've been thinking about that,' Stan said. 'I think there might be two reasons. One is that he might be intending to go back to sea. He doesn't like leaving people onshore, not unless he can spare a group of four or more. He reckons singletons and even pairs can start getting ideas into their heads. Haines likes to keep close track of his people. You never know who you can trust and he makes sure it stays that way. But I think the real reason might be that he's over-stretched. When I first got out I followed some of his people around for a while. Some I knew, but on separate occasions I counted four in all that I'd not seen before.'

'That doesn't mean they're new to the organization,' Mac argued. 'You've been gone for a while.'

'True, but you get to know how people behave around those they don't know yet, don't really know if they can rely upon. It's not just with a group like Haines runs. It's in the army, it's everywhere. People act different around people they know well enough to watch their backs.'

It was an interesting theory, Mac thought, and if it was true that Haines was adding to the size of his operation, it kind of fitted with the idea that Haines and Vaschinsky were looking to increase their influence.

'That note you found. Any ideas?'

Stan shook his head and grimaced with pain. 'No, but there's only a couple of people had the opportunity to put it in my pocket. Santos and Jerry, and my money's on Jerry.'

'Any particular reason?'

'Santos is Haines's man through and through. Been with him ten years or more.'

'And Jerry Mason?'

'Longer than me. About three years, maybe a bit less. Don't know a lot about him, though. He was the quiet type. What Haines said, he did. Thick as pudding. Liked to take pictures, though. Knew all about cameras.'

'What kind of pictures?'

Stan laughed and then very obviously wished he hadn't. 'Oh nothing like that. Landscape, mostly. Architecture. It was a bit of a joke. Not that you'd say anything to his face. Not if you didn't want a fist in yours.'

Mac thought about that and what Kendall had told him earlier about their being an undercover officer in Haines's crew. Assuming this Jerry was their man on the inside, what made him so sure that Stan would find his message and pass it along? If he was any good at his job—and if he'd survived for three years, Mac had to assume he was—then presumably he'd know a bit about Stan Holden and where he was staying, and so guess there was a chance the message, whatever it was, would end up in the right hands. It seemed a little desperate, though.

'There's one thing I don't get,' he said.

Stan lay back against the arm of the sofa. He looked bone weary. 'And what's that?'

'If Haines wanted you to be effective against Karen—I mean, even assuming that would be possible—then why leave you in such bad shape? My bet is you can barely make it to the front door, never mind go haring off after psychopathic young women.'

Stan smiled weakly. 'I think you'll find she's a sociopath,' he said. 'Not that I like to split hairs, but it strikes me she's too capable of love and passion and all that crap to qualify as a psychopath. And as to the shape I'm in? Santos thought he'd add a few more bruises of his own after the boss had finished with me. Santos and I never did get along and he's not the sort to play nice.'

'Even if his boss wants you out there working for him?'

Stan was clearly amused, but just as clearly too much in pain to laugh now. 'Santos knows I don't have a cat in hell's against Karen,' Stan said, 'and Haines knows it too, he's just amusing himself. It's what he does.'

He closed his eyes and Mac recognized he wouldn't get anything more out of him that morning.

Rina met him in the hall. 'Anything useful?'

'Oh, bits and bobs. It's hard to know at this stage. When do you see Karen's solicitor?'

'Monday afternoon.'

'Good. Look, I've got to get going. I'll give you a call later on.'

'And what arrangements have you made to look after George? If Haines goes after him—'

'I think that was just leverage. But I'm looking out for him, I promise. Let me know what the solicitor says.'

Rina nodded and saw him out. She was a little disappointed, truth be told, that Mac did not appear to be taking the Karen situation and the threat to George more seriously.

She went through to where Stan was now dozing on the sofa and woke him up.

'How seriously do you view this threat to George?' she demanded.

Stan groaned. 'Rina, I don't know.' He took one look at her expression and decided he needed to do better than that. Painfully, he eased himself up into a sitting position. 'Like I just said to Mac, I don't think Karen's a high priority, more of a bonus, and George, well, my guess is that at the moment Haines will hold off. He'll wait, see what I do, see what Karen does. If we do nothing then he might decide to use George as incentive, but to be truthful, Rina, I never knew how to read the man. He conforms to his own pattern.'

Rina sat down in the fireside chair close to the sofa and leaned forward earnestly. 'Stan, I need advice here. What should we do?'

He sighed. 'What I had planned was to find Karen. The way I see it she probably knows more about the game that's being played here than either we or that policeman of yours do. Frankly, I think I'd then let her call the shots. I don't care if she kills Haines or any bugger else associated with him. I don't much care if he gets to her first, but I do care about the boy. It seems to me he's been through enough grief.'

'Mac seems unwilling to do much.'

Stan shook his head. 'Rina, he's not going to tell you what his plans are, not while I'm living here. Far as Mac's concerned I'm still the enemy. Oh, he may not show it, maybe doesn't even think it, but we've been on opposite sides for so long he's bound to act like it. So he won't tell you anything you might accidentally let slip and tell me. Don't judge him, that's just the way things are and he cares about what happens to young George just the way you do.'

Rina nodded. 'I suppose you're right,' she said. 'I'm constantly putting him in an awkward position. The solicitor must have some means of getting in touch with Karen,' she reasoned. 'He's got to be our best bet. I suppose I ought to be careful what I tell Mac about that too. He's not going to like me being involved.'

'You'll have to figure that one out as you go along,' Stan said. 'And let's hope the solicitor has a means of contacting Karen, because frankly, Rina, I think I'm bugger all use to anyone right now.'

TWENTY-FIVE

A couple of days later, Andy let himself into the tiny police station on Frantham promenade. At the height of the holiday season it was usual for the office to be manned on a Sunday; Frank Baker, Andy and a couple of community support officers shared the duty on a rota system, but by September there was very little need. Andy closed the door and slipped into the office he shared with Frank.

So, it was another Sunday; he could have gone to his mother's place or out with friends, but Andy knew he'd not be able to settle until he'd dealt with the next step in the investigation.

He needed to talk to the people who had really known Kath Eebry at the time of her disappearance, and that meant sifting through all the statements and interviews and media publicity that had been generated back then.

There was a depressing amount; on the other hand it meant that many people had cared about Kath.

She had a sister, it seemed. Andy hadn't known about her. He jotted down the phone number and address and wondered why Ted and the girls had never mentioned her, or at least not that he could remember. There were a couple of work colleagues that had come forward with concerns, and one, a Terry Birch, had actually been the one to report Kath Eebry missing, worried she'd not been to work for a few days and had not been answering calls.

Andy read the statement carefully. This Terry Birch had been concerned enough to actually go round to the Eebry house, only to find the family departed on what turned out to be an extended holiday.

Was he the man Kath had been seeing? Two other work colleagues had come forward with their worries and both said that Kath had seemed anxious in the days before she disappeared. Andy realized he didn't really know what Kath Eebry did. It looked, from the statements, that it was some kind of administration at a private language college in Exeter. She'd been there long enough for the other staff to regard her as a valued friend, that much was clear. And with Ted being self-employed, a regular wage would have been a useful thing, Andy reckoned.

'So, when you lost that, how did you pay the mortgage, Ted? You only worked school hours, far as I can remember,' Andy murmured. And in the summer, although he had taken the girls along with him to auctions and they had accompanied him to the markets, it must have been difficult juggling earning with childcare.

Andy flicked through the statements again, recalling something one of them had said. Someone else had asked that exact same question. And the investigating officer had asked Ted Eebry. The answer was a simple one. There hadn't been a mortgage. Kath Eebry had paid for the house out of the sale of her parents' place when they had died.

Andy went through the documents and added to his list of names and numbers and addresses. Recalling his misadventures doing house to house earlier that week, he groaned at the thought of working through this lot, but needs must. That was what he was going to have to do.

TWENTY-SIX

On late Monday morning, Andy contrived to 'bump into' Stacey on her way home from the local play-group. He knew her schedule, because he had bumped into her for real on the odd occasion.

He bent down to make a fuss of the little girl strapped into her buggy. 'Hello, Tammy. Ah, who's this?' he asked as she presented him with a rather lopsided teddy bear. The ears were soggy where she'd been chewing on them.

Tammy giggled.

'He's just called Ted,' Stacey said. 'Like her toy cat and her favourite cushion. Everything she really likes is named after her grandad.'

Andy winced. He hoped she hadn't noticed. He got up and fell into step beside her.

'I hear you saw him?'

'Yes, we had a cup of tea.'

'And you asked about Mum.'

'Yes. Stacey, I—'

'It's all right. Dad said you were just doing your job. He said you were really embarrassed about it.'

That was one way of putting it. Andy managed a smile. 'It seemed really odd,' he admitted. 'How come he's moving?'

'Oh, I guess the bullying paid off in the end.' She smiled. 'It's for his own good. At least, I hope it is,' she said with a laugh. 'I know he wants to be closer. He dotes on Tammy and that place is far too big for him now. He's just rattling around there in a house full of memories and not all of them good—' She broke off and looked away from Andy. Then carried on, 'Hardest thing was finding somewhere he could afford with a big enough garden. You know what he's like with his garden.'

'And have you found somewhere?'

'Yes, a bungalow about ten minutes' walk from us, nice garden and good views. Of course he's got to get his place sold first, and things aren't shifting very fast. It's not the sort of place to appeal to the second-home brigade and it's too expensive for first-time buyers, so I guess we'll just have to hope that a family will like it and not mind that it's out there on its own and in a lousy catchment area for schools—and that the bungalow is still on the market when the time comes.'

'He does have a really big garden,' Andy remembered.

'Yeah. It was when the company that was going to build the estate went bust and the rest of the estate wasn't going to get built after all, I think the receivers said did the residents want to buy up some land. I suppose it was a way of getting some money back for the creditors. Anyway, Dad bought that big chunk going down to the field boundary. You know, the bit he called his allotment, near the wildlife pond.'

Andy remembered. The pond had actually been on the farm side, but the field was fallow and used only for grazing so no one minded the kids going pond dipping. Ted had grown fruit and veg and all manner of stuff. More than his own family could eat. Andy had often gone home with carrier bags full of fresh veg. It had been a very welcome addition when things were short.

'Didn't he keep chickens for a while?'

'Abigail and Bertha, yes. They were never very good layers and a fox got Bertha and that did for Abigail. Turned up her claws and died a week later.' She laughed.

'There was that great big smelly compost heap,' Andy remembered. 'Near the pond. Your dad reckoned there were newts living in it.'

'Oh, there were. He showed me. It was a lovely garden. Lovely childhood, really, despite, well, you know.'

Andy nodded. 'He said she'd gone off with someone,' he told Stacey.

She halted. Turned to look at him in surprise. 'He said that?'

'Yes.'

'No!' She laughed and walked on. 'No one ever thought that. Something happened to her. She couldn't come home because something bad had happened. She'd never just go.'

No, Andy thought sadly. He didn't reckon she would either, but he also found it impossible to see Ted Eebry as any kind of killer. None of it seemed right.

* * *

Andy spent the rest of the morning on the phone. As would be expected after all this time, many of the names and numbers were either unobtainable or owned by someone else. He struck lucky with the college, though. The language school still existed and there was a woman there who could remember Kath Eebry. Theresa Leary had been the receptionist back then and was now chief administrator.

'She was a lovely lady. Very sweet and calm and got along so well with the students.'

'What exactly was her job?' Andy asked.

'Well it was sort of the precursor to mine, I suppose. The language school was smaller then, just two floors and four classrooms, we're double that now. Kath looked after things like arranging accommodation, sorting out financial problems, making sure the students knew how to get around the city and that sort of thing, and on top of that she managed the diary for all the teaching staff. We've always used part timers, so she kept on top of who was doing what and made sure they submitted their time sheets and all that sort of stuff. It was mostly routine, but she was really organized,'

'And well liked. I get the impression from the statements that she was popular.'

'Well yes, from what I can remember she was. It was easy to like Kath, she was always happy and cheerful and would do anything she could to help out.'

'Are you in touch with anyone else from back then?'

He felt the hesitation. 'Does this mean you've found her?'

'I've been given a batch of cold cases to work through,' Andy said. It was close enough to the truth.

'But you must have something new?'

'I'm sorry,' Andy said. 'I can't really comment, you understand.'

A second or two of silence. 'I see,' she said, though it was clear from her tone that Theresa Leary really didn't.

'Other members of staff?' Andy prompted.

It turned out she was still in contact with two. One was a teacher and probably wouldn't remember Kath well. Andy took the details anyway; it was not a name he already had on his list, so worth a try. The second was Terry Birch, the man who had reported Kath missing in the first place. Andy could have cheered.

TWENTY-SEVEN

When Karen had told Vaschinsky she had two killings in mind, she had not been joking. It had taken her a while to get access to this second man, another associate of her father's in times gone by, because he'd been in jail.

Out for three weeks now, he was the final element; the one thing left to do before she went away. He'd been living in a halfway house, this last target of hers, but had just moved into a bedsit at the top of a three-storey building in a very rundown area. It was a long way from Frantham; truth be known it was in Vashinsky's territory, but that didn't bother Karen. Brig Morten was not the sort of man Vaschinsky or anyone else was going to be bothered about.

She could remember him from very early in her child-hood, from even before George came on the scene. She could remember the smell of him: beer and cigarettes and an odd overlay of wet dog and what her dad had called funny fags. And she could remember his hands: calloused on the palms from the weights he used to lift and tattooed across the backs and knuckles. He was younger than her dad, and if anything even more vicious, and Karen knew this was not going to be as easy as David Jenkins had been.

She sat on the very edge of his bed in the dingy little room, waiting for him to return. Beneath her feet she could hear the banging and clattering of the tenant a floor below. He'd been playing music when Karen let herself in—the lock on the door was scarcely deserving of the name—but he'd been shouted at to turn it down about an hour ago, and after a brief argument had complied. Karen had heard the sound of knuckles meeting flesh and a great deal of swearing in the aftermath. She knew that all the men in this building were ex-cons. It was a dumping ground for those kicked out of the hostel after two weeks and who had no family or friends to take them in.

Karen and George and their—she hesitated to call them parents—had lived in a great many such places over the years. She had learnt early to stay quiet, to stay curled up in the middle of the bed with her books and her toys and the packed lunch her mum made her before she went out. Karen had taught George to stay quiet too. To be invisible, to pretend they weren't there. She'd been good at that, and in a way that was why she was here. It was to lay a memory to rest; an incident that stood out so vividly in her mind that Karen had known the only way she could excise it was to excise the man himself.

She knew she'd have to be quiet now, to be quick and clean and not give him time to call for help. She wondered if anyone would come if he did anyway; in a place like this it was hard to believe that anyone could give a damn about anyone else. They never had in Karen's experience.

But *she'd* given a damn. About herself and her mother and George, and that was all that mattered really. That and the chance to finally remove this last bad thing. Then, she felt, she could let go. Be free.

Karen looked again around the tiny, sordid little room. Set at the top of the house with a high dormer window looking out at the sky, the walls had been papered and painted over so many times the covering was now the thickness of cardboard. Out of curiosity, Karen picked away at a loose fragment and counted the layers, peeling them off one at a time. She counted ten and there were others still on the wall. Floorboards covered with threadbare carpet offered little protection from the splintered timber, and the bed was a narrow single, sagging at the springs and made up with cheap sheets and thin blankets. An unzipped sleeping bag spread across the top afforded some small comfort. If you didn't feel like cutting your wrists before you came to stay here, Karen thought, you sure as hell would living in this place.

It made her wonder just how she and George had survived. Somehow, they had always believed that life could be better, and as soon as she'd been old enough and capable enough to make stuff happen, things really had started to improve.

'Work hard,' she had always told him. 'Don't be like *them*. Believe you can be better.'

Karen had searched the bedsit when she had first arrived but had found very little: spare clothes, a penknife, which she had slipped into her pocket, the bare minimum in the way of toiletries in the sparse bathroom. Magazines stuffed beneath the pillow which she had left alone despite the fact that she was wearing latex gloves. No food in the cupboards and only beer in the tiny fridge. A couple of pizza boxes stuffed in the bin were the only evidence that the man actually ate. A fire escape led down from the kitchen and she had checked that it would open. It did, but the cast-iron steps looked older and in worse shape than the house.

Best be prepared, though. It had been the first thing Karen had done wherever they had been: check for possible escape routes. She had taught George to do the same and she wondered if it was a habit he'd kept up.

She could still leave now. Walk away. No one would be any the wiser.

Karen knew full well that she might need more than a rusty fire escape to get her out of this one. She touched the handgun that lay on the bed beside her. Dave Jenkins had been little challenge, really. Brig Morten was something else again, and for once in her life Karen was less than certain she could achieve what she had set out to do.

She heard the front door crash open and strained to hear footsteps on the stairs. Twice now she'd heard the door open and twice been disappointed. But not this time.

Heavy footsteps on the stairs, stomping along the landing, coming up to the top floor. Karen moved off the bed and took up position just inside the door so that it would conceal her when he first opened it. She hoped he didn't crash that half off its hinges the way he'd done with the front door. She clasped the gun lightly and easily, calmed her breathing. She had no qualms about shooting this man in the back; she figured she'd need all the advantages she could get and, after all, the man had no qualms about attacking those who could not protect themselves.

Like he'd attacked her mother. Like she had no doubt he would have attacked her.

Stay quiet, don't move, don't say a word. Karen could so vividly remember what her mother had said, how she had sounded, and how she had pushed Karen into the cupboard only seconds before Brig Morten came through the door, drunk as usual and intent on only one thing.

Don't let him know you're there.

And Karen could so vividly remember how she had hidden her face and crammed her fists into her mouth and bitten down hard enough for it to hurt, but she hadn't made a sound while Brig Morten raped her mother only yards away.

Now he seemed to pause outside the door and she wondered if he suspected something, but a moment later he slid the key into the lock, fumbling the operation twice before completing it. He swung the door wide and stepped over the threshold, then paused again, sniffing this time, like some massive old hound. He could smell her, she thought. The only clean thing in this filthy room.

Then two things happened very fast. Brig grabbed the door and slammed it closed and Karen fired, hitting him in the gut.

Brig Morten staggered back, momentarily surprised. He stared at her and she saw the recognition dawn. Karen fired again, this time aiming for a head shot, but Brig was far from finished. He snarled, launched his full weight towards her. Karen side stepped and her shot went wide, grazing his shoulder, deflecting him for a split second before he came again.

Karen swore softly. She was exactly where she did not want to be now, wedged between the door and the bed and the man mountain about to throw himself on her.

Karen knew she had one chance. She did not fire again. She waited. In reality it was less than seconds, but that waiting time seemed to stretch beyond all reality. She knew this was the only way, knew also that she had, quite literally, just the one chance to get it right this time.

He grabbed her hair, tugging her head back, then went for the gun hand. Karen could feel his breath on her face, feel the spittle as he panted with the sudden exertion. He was bleeding heavily but nothing seemed to slow him down. Karen had expected that. Nothing ever slowed Brig Morten down.

That sense of stretched time seemed even more acute. His hand was about to close over hers, but she snatched it away. Her final shot was upward through his lower jaw, not at quite the angle Karen would have liked, but it did the job. As he began to fall, Karen pushed hard, deflecting the body away from her and skittering away into the corner before leaping on to the bed. She stood there, poised above the man, still not sure, in spite of the fact that the top of his head was absent from the rest, that he was actually dead.

He didn't move.

The noise of Brig Morten crashing down on to his bedsit floor had aroused the ire of the tenant below. Karen could hear him shouting and cursing. Without another glance she hopped off the bed and out through the kitchen, down the fire escape. She tucked the gun into her raincoat pocket and removed the coat and latex gloves. She had blood on her black trousers and just a little on her dark T-shirt. She folded her coat so that the mess was concealed on the inside, barely pausing in her headlong flight down the rusted stairs. A shout from the room she had just vacated evidenced the fact that the tenant below had done more than shout at Brig Morten through the floor.

Karen loped down the last flight and ran out of the yard and between the houses. Then she slowed down, walked at a moderate pace to the end of the road and only then did she risk looking back. Nothing. No one in pursuit.

Could have been worse, Karen thought, adrenalin still surging through her body. She turned right at the end of the road and slipped into an alleyway she had scouted earlier, between two rows of houses. Rubbish was out for collection and soon Karen's coat and gloves and gun had joined it, stuffed in a black plastic bag and then into a half-empty wheelie bin. Then she walked on to where she'd left her car, an odd feeling of emptiness mingled with relief replacing the adrenalin.

Now what? Karen Parker thought.

TWENTY-EIGHT

Andy had managed to make an appointment with Terry Birch for three thirty that Monday afternoon. He was working as a full-time primary teacher now and finished around three.

'Come to the school,' Terry said. 'We can chat before I drive home. If that's OK?'

St Anne's Primary was the sort of village school that had only a few dozen kids, one teacher and a headmistress. Terry met him in the yard and showed him through to the office.

'Sit yourself down. This is about Kath?'

Andy nodded cautiously. 'Mr Birch, can I ask you something? Your relationship with Kath Eebry—'

Terry Birch hesitated. 'We had a brief affair,' he said. 'I don't think anyone knew about it. I loved her very much but she loved her husband and kids more. We decided it would be better if we broke things off. So she did. Next thing I know, Kath had gone.'

'*You* reported her missing and not her husband.'

Terry nodded. 'She didn't turn up for work. That wasn't like her. She hadn't called in sick, she'd not been in touch at all. None of that was right, not for Kath, she was far too considerate, far too conscientious for that.'

'Did you try and call her?'

'I did, and the principal at the school, Dan Ingrams, he called her too, but there was no reply. In the end I called round. A neighbour told me Ted and the kids had gone away but that no one had seen Kath and she hadn't been with them. Ted Eebry had told them she'd gone away.'

'And how long after you decided to break it off was that?'

'About a week. We met one last time for a drink. Nowhere local, we didn't risk that, and we talked things over and decided it couldn't go on. It was fair to no one, least of all me or the kids.'

'And did you see her at all after that?'

Terry nodded. 'At work. We met on the Wednesday evening. She worked Wednesday evenings and we stole a half hour after that. She came in on the Thursday and the Friday. She said the kids were going out with some friends at the weekend, I think. I said goodbye to her on the Friday afternoon and I never saw her again.'

'Kath had a sister. Did she ever talk about her? Did you not think she might have gone there?'

Terry shook his head. 'They didn't get along,' he said. 'I don't know all the details. Kath didn't talk about her a lot. When their parents died, and I think they were both gone within a year, everything was divided between the two sisters. Kath, I think, invested most of her share in the house she and Ted bought. She said her sister got through her share in a couple of years and came looking for more. Kath told her where to go. It's funny, she could be so soft with everyone else, but Jean just got up her nose.'

'What happened to the sister—do you know?'

'Um, someone told me she died a couple of years after Kath disappeared. She was an alcoholic. Kath always reckoned she would never make old bones.'

'And what do you think happened to Kath Eebry?'

Terry shook his head. 'What I always thought,' he said. 'Ted found out about us and he killed her. I'll never forgive myself, or him, for that.'

* * *

Mac had reported back to Kendall what Stan had said and what had happened to him.

'You've taken a formal statement?'

Mac laughed. 'No, and I doubt he'd agree to make one. We're not likely to be bringing charges, are we?'

'We could try.'

'Oh sure, we bring Haines in on a GBH charge and see how many minutes it doesn't take his solicitor to make fools of us. You'd not get Stan to testify. He wants to hang on to what life he's got left.'

Kendall sighed. 'And this threat to young George Parker?'

'I don't know. It may just be rhetoric. Haines has it in for Karen. She's crossed him a few too many times.' He paused, trying to remember exactly what Kendall knew about Karen. There was a lot that wasn't public currency, even among his colleagues, for reasons that had seemed good at the time but now seemed less than wise.

'I've heard a lot of rumours about her,' Kendall said. 'Most seem implausible. She's violent, though? Anyway, her brother is the concern here. You'll talk to him?'

'I'll make sure I see him later on,' Mac said. 'Extra patrols up around Hill House wouldn't come amiss, and a safe house?'

Kendall laughed. 'I'll do what I can,' he said.

Mac was sure he would, but knew that wasn't likely to be much. The threat was too vague and had emerged from too unreliable a source.

'Perhaps put a watch on George,' he said. 'He's pretty safe while he's in school and extra patrols would help up at

Hill House. Let them know something is up, but tell them not to alert George. He's had enough of being the centre of attention. It's the walk from the college to where the minibus picks them up that's the real danger point.'

'Mac, I'm already fighting for resources.'

'And if any of Haines's men try to make contact? Worst case scenario is that Haines actually carries out his threat. Where's that going to leave you? Worse off than just fighting for resources. Stan might not be happy making a formal statement, but I can sure as hell put this conversation on record. Information received of a viable threat.'

Kendall frowned, but Mac could see he was taking this on board. 'I'll do what I can,' he said. 'That's all I can say.'

'That'll have to do then,' Mac said.

TWENTY-NINE

Andy had headed back to Frantham and was taking another look at the photographs of the bones from the dig site and at the report the pathologist had sent through. It seemed too vague—approximation of age, a guess at sex; it bothered Andy that they were still not one hundred per cent even about that. The bones were gracile, estimated height around five feet five inches, so probably female.

Wasn't this meant to be a more exact science?

Most puzzling for Andy were the marks that had been observed on the tibia. Back at the dig site, Elodie had mentioned them and wondered if they were shallow cut marks, but closer inspection showed them to be criss-crossed by others, so that an uneven grid had been marked out on the bone. The pathologist had speculated that something had been on the body as it decomposed, that something had pressed down through the layers of flesh until it came to rest against the bone.

Andy felt he needed more. He needed something definite in this morass of might bes and could bes and probably isn'ts.

He hesitated before calling Miriam, knowing that his boss's girlfriend hadn't been working as a CSI since late the previous year, so she definitely didn't qualify as official channels. Where she did qualify was that she was something of an expert on bones.

Andy stared at the pictures. He could hear Frank Baker in the front office chatting to a woman about yet another lost dog. Hadn't people heard of leads? The number of holidaymakers who let their dogs run on the beach unsupervised every year astounded Andy. In his experience dogs not used to the sea often freaked and ran. It stood to reason, he thought. However big and noisy the dog, the sea was going to be bigger and noisier.

Mac was off somewhere doing something on the other murder enquiry no doubt—the 'more important because we've got a proper body' enquiry—and so Andy figured it was his call. He picked up the phone and called Miriam Hastings.

* * *

'Miss Munroe said you might have some concerns, so I'd like to assure you I'm here and available to answer any questions. And in the years to come, provision has been made for you to make use of our services should you require them—you or George Parker.'

Munroe, thought Rina. She had seen the signature on the documents but it still seemed strange to hear the solicitor using that name. 'Did Miss Munroe say why she wanted me to be her executor?'

'She said she knew you well and trusted you. That you were an old family friend.' He looked discomforted, but then so did most people when they had dealings with Karen, Rina thought. She nodded agreement and he looked a little more relieved.

'May I ask where this money comes from?'

'Of course. Look, the paperwork is all very clear and simple. A relative of Miss Munroe left her a great deal of money. Perhaps you know the Canadian branch of the family?'

Rina did not. She doubted they existed.

'Well Miss Munroe is obviously a very generous young woman. She was aware that the elderly relative, a Miss Simmonds, didn't know about young George. She was sure that if she had been aware then some bequest would have been forthcoming and so she took it upon herself to fulfil that role.' He looked grave for a moment and then said, 'She explained about the divisions within the family, that George's family and hers had, shall we say, become estranged over time.' He leaned forward across the desk. 'I understand that George's mother made a rather bad marriage and the family cut her off.'

'You could say that,' Rina agreed. 'It's been painful for everyone concerned.'

'I can imagine. So because of that and because she lives abroad, she thought you could take over the role of executor of the trust, alongside ourselves, of course.'

'Of course. So what exactly do I have to do?'

'Ah, well.' He smiled, on much firmer ground now. 'I've prepared a portfolio for you, so you can study the assets, and I've taken the liberty of drawing up a rough plan. As you'll see, George is entitled to a small allowance now, and then when he is eighteen a slice of the capital. The remainder will be made over to him at ages twenty-one and twenty-seven. All you really have to do is be an adviser to the young man. Answer any immediate questions he might have, and attend a meeting here once a year to discuss interest on the capital and how to reinvest that amount.'

'Interest?' Rina asked. 'How much interest?'

He clearly thought it was a slightly odd question, given all those she might have asked, but he said, 'I estimate about twenty-five thousand pounds a year at current rates. Of course, all funds are being invested in low to moderate risk bonds, Miss Munroe was quite explicit about that, even though our financial department advised her that she could get a far better return.'

Rina blinked. So how much was this estate worth? She didn't want to ask. She'd rather just sit down with this portfolio of his, somewhere quiet and where she had access to a half-bottle of brandy or at least a pot of strong tea. Just what the hell had Karen been up to?

Rina wasn't sure she wanted to know, but there was a question she just had to ask. 'This relative that died. You're sure it's all above board? I mean, you hear such dreadful things. Such cruel scams.'

The solicitor smiled. 'We, of course, wondered about that. We commissioned private detectives both here and in Canada and spoke to the firm dealing with the estate over there and all the relevant tax authorities. Miss Munroe financed that of course, so you don't need to be concerned about that.'

'I see,' Rina said. 'And you don't think it a strange thing to do? To make over all of this money to a boy she can scarcely know?'

'Of course we wondered about that too. As you say, there are so many schemes and scams and criminal activities going on, but we commissioned our own investigation into Miss Munroe. She lives in France for most of the year, was educated in Paris and Lyon and speaks several languages. She lives very quietly, very respectably.'

Respectably, Rina thought. Karen. Who the hell had she created for them to investigate?

'And is it possible for you to contact her? Is there a phone number I could have?'

'I'm sorry, Mrs Martin, but she specified there should be no direct contact either from you or the boy. I do, of course, have a number I can call to leave a message. I think she anticipated that you might wish to do this.'

Rina nodded. 'Could you tell her,' she said, 'that of course I will look after George. It will be my pleasure, but could you also tell her that an old acquaintance, Mr Haines, has been in touch, and as she's leaving soon she may just want to deal with that before she goes.'

The solicitor looked puzzled. 'Will she understand that? Does she need a phone number or anything?'

'She'll understand. It's a minor matter, but I'm sure she'll want to get it sorted out.'

She smiled sweetly at the solicitor who was clearly thinking that something odd was going on here, but he couldn't quite work out what or how concerned he ought to be.

'Now what was it you wanted me to sign?'

THIRTY

The little coffee shop on the promenade had been the location for many meetings and odd conversations. This Tuesday morning, Andy chose a discreet table in the corner where he and Miriam could sit undisturbed and passed the folder across to her.

For a while she sipped coffee and studied the photographs and reports in silence, a small frown creasing her brow and the bridge of her nose. Andy watched a little anxiously. He wasn't sure if Miriam would be able to help; was equally unsure if he actually wanted her to say anything definitive. Anything that might add to the weight of suspicion now bearing down on him.

Anxious too that Mac might disapprove. Mac was anxious about anything that might distress Miriam.

She finally shuffled everything together and looked brightly at Andy. He breathed a sigh of relief.

'So,' she said, 'what can I tell you?'

'Well,' Andy said slowly. 'I know there's not a lot to go on.'

'Not a great deal, no. A skull would be helpful, but going with what we do have, I agree with what's in the report. The ends of the long bone are fully fused, so the likelihood

174

is this is a person older than, say, twenty-five, but with the lack of any significant age-related wear, well, I'd say younger than fifty.'

Andy nodded. 'How long would it take for a body to rot?' he asked.

'Um, depends on the circumstances. In a hot country you could get full skeletonization within, say, a couple of weeks.' She paused, frowning. 'How much do you know about any of this?'

'Not a lot,' Andy admitted. 'I mean, how would you conceal something like that? Dead bodies smell . . .'

Miriam laughed. 'True,' she said. 'But you can minimize that. I heard about a body left wrapped in industrial cling film. The neighbours noticed a bad smell but thought it was the drains. Putrefaction causes a terrible stink, but the worst of it is over in a relatively short time.'

'How short? Say, if I'd buried something in the garden.'

'You only have a flat,' Miriam observed. 'And I think your mother would notice if you dug up her flower beds.' She looked quizzically at him. 'Do you have something specific in mind?'

'I don't know,' Andy admitted. 'I'm really not sure.'

'Ookay. Right. Well let's start with the basics. Buried or unburied?'

'I think buried.'

'Disturbed?' She tapped the folder. 'Judging from the state of these bones I'd say probably not.'

'Probably not then. Miriam, can you tell how long they'd been buried?'

'Not just from looking at these pictures. You see there's no context, just a few bones thrown into a trench. I really wouldn't like to make a better guess than my old colleagues have in the report.'

'OK.' Andy had known this but was still disappointed. 'So if the body had been buried?'

'That would slow things down. Decomposition would still take place and there'd be some insect activity. Fly strike can literally happen within minutes of death. Then there'd be the action of worms and micro-organisms in the soil and so on.'

'But would neighbours, say, smell the decomp?'

'Um, well, it would depend how close they got and how deep the body was buried. Look, what happens in general terms is this. Decomp starts pretty quickly and the first stage lasts maybe four to ten days, depending on where the body is and factors like temperature. Rigor sets in after a few hours, but by that time the body is already starting to rot from the inside out. It literally starts to digest itself. The first stage, when the digestive enzymes start to break down cell walls, well that starts within a few hours and lasts maybe three or four days. As you know, you also get the blood dropping down to the lowest point of the body. In fact, that can start as soon as an hour or two after death. Chances are, a body could be quite close by and you'd not notice much out of the ordinary.'

'So at what point—'

'Might the neighbours notice the smell? Well, putre-faction proper starts roughly between day four and day ten after death. Gases build up, the body bloats, tissues start to break down. Then you get what we call black putrefaction, which lasts roughly until day twenty-five or so. You've got to remember, Andy, a lot of this depends on exposure and temperature. Bloating subsides and the skin blackens and starts to peel away. What you smell then is butyric acid, not just the results of bloating and body fluids. You OK?'

Andy nodded. He knew Miriam was just trying to help, but a picture had started to form in his mind of Kath Eebry, not just dead but rotting and falling away into the earth. The woman he had known disfigured by the process of death and complete decay.

'And then what?'

'And then we get the drying stage. It starts sometime between the twenty-fifth and fiftieth day, but it can take any anything up to a year, after which you'll be left with bones and hair and maybe a little dried skin.' She shrugged. 'That's just one very basic scenario. It would seem to fit what we have, but—'

'And what do you make of this?' Andy shuffled through the photographs until he found the image of the bone with the strange marks. 'At first it looked like maybe marks from a knife or something, but—'

Miriam shook her head. 'No, I don't think those are cut marks. I think they're caused by pressure. Something pressing down on the body as it decomposed, then the pressure of, say, soil gradually becoming more intense as the flesh rots away and whatever caused the pattern finally coming to rest on the bone.' She frowned. 'There seems to be some slight discolouration in and around the indentations, but that might just be an artefact on the image. I'd need to see the bone itself. Has anyone run any tests?'

'I don't think so,' Andy said. 'Whoever she is—was—she's kind of at the back of the queue right now.'

Miriam nodded sympathetically. 'Limited resources,' she said. 'Everything has to be prioritized. If you had a positive ID then she'd move up the line.' She studied Andy carefully. 'Do you think you know who she was?'

He shrugged self-consciously. 'I think, right now, I don't want to know,' he said. 'Oh, don't worry, I'll run down every lead I can find. I'll do my job, it's just . . .'

'Andy, have you talked to Mac about this? You don't have to do this on your own. Far from it. If you think you may have a personal connection . . . is that what you're saying?'

'I think . . . Look, I have talked to Mac. Not his fault, but he's got a lot on his plate at the moment apart from this and I don't want to let him down.'

Miriam was amused at the thought. 'Mac knows you wouldn't,' she said. 'But you are a team, you know, and there's such a thing as *him* letting *you* down too. He'd be horrified to think he was doing that.'

'Yeah, I know.' Andy sipped the rest of his coffee. It was cold now and suddenly seemed too sweet. 'Thanks, Miriam, you've been a big help. Want another coffee?'

'Love one, and how about we talk about something else for a while.'

Andy nodded and got up to get their drinks. He was aware of Miriam's gaze following him as he crossed the little café, and knew she was right. He did feel oddly let down and horribly alone, but he also knew that he had to be the one to see this through. That this wasn't a burden he was ready to share.

* * *

'We'll have to stop meeting like this,' George joked wryly as he spotted Mac waiting for them. 'You'll be getting us a reputation.'

Mac smiled. In actual fact he always waited at a distance from the college, not wanting to cause additional complications for George and Ursula, but he was relieved at the tone of the greeting; he had not parted from George on the best of terms.

Ursula smiled shyly at him. She looked pale, he thought, and anxious. He wondered what was wrong.

'So?'

'So we've got a problem,' Mac said. Beating about the bush didn't seem very appropriate right now.

'With?'

Where to start. 'With your dad's old boss, Haines. He had his men pick Stan up off the street and beat seven shades out of him.'

'Is he OK?' George touched Mac's arm, emphasizing the level of his concern. George rarely volunteered physical contact, even with those he knew well.

'He's OK, back at Peverill Lodge and being pampered as you might expect.'

Ursula laughed and George relaxed a little. Mac could tell he was pleased to see Ursula happier, even momentarily.

'What did he do that for?' George asked.

'He wanted Stan to do something and Stan wasn't very willing. George, I think you should go away for a few days. I can arrange a place today and we can soon clear it with Hill House.'

The teenagers halted and looked at him and then at one another. 'No,' George said, and in a tone that told Mac this was final. That he'd have to pick him up and physically take him away to change his mind.

'George, I don't think you understand.'

'Then you'd better tell me, but the answer will still be no.'

'Ursula—'

'Mac, don't even bother.'

They walked on and Mac took a deep breath. 'It seems your sister's back,' he said.

George stiffened but walked on at the same pace.

'There's something big going down between Haines and another major player. It's possible Karen is mixed up in that somehow. Haines wanted Stan to go after her, to—'

'Kill her?' George laughed. 'Like that's really going to happen.'

'Stan refused, so Haines threatened to get to Karen through you. I'm sorry, George, but I really think—'

'No.'

'I could—'

'Make me?' George halted and swung round to face Mac. 'Look, if he's after me he'll get to me wherever. You know that as well as I do. I'm tired of running, Mac. I did it most of my life and I'm not doing it now. Haines wants me he can come and get me, but I'm not hiding out just because I happen to be someone's son or someone's brother.'

The teenagers walked on stiff-backed and Mac followed them.

'George, you have to think about other people. You could be putting others at risk.'

He was not prepared for the surge of anger which George turned on him.

'Don't you try and blackmail me. Don't you try and make me feel bad. You don't have a clue, do you, don't know a fucking thing about me. I grew up being blackmailed. With people forcing me to do what they wanted. My dad used his fists, but my mum was just as bad, kept me just as scared, and Karen. Karen . . .' He broke off and Mac could see that he was fighting tears. 'Always bloody Karen.'

Ursula had hold of him, her arms tight around him as George hid his face in her shoulder, his entire body shaking. She did not even look at Mac.

Slowly, George calmed and pulled away. Ursula laid her hands against his cheeks, cupping his face. He leaned towards her, forehead resting on hers as she wiped tears away. Mac stood apart, at a loss and completely excluded. He wanted to tell them that it would all be OK, that in the end everything could turn out right, but he didn't want to be caught in a lie.

'George, I'm sorry,' Mac said.

'I think you should go,' Ursula told him, but there was no anger in her voice, just more sorrow, Mac thought, than any girl of fifteen should ever have to know.

THIRTY-ONE

Andy had gone home and changed his clothes, looked to see what he had in his fridge and decided he didn't fancy any of it. He needed to get out for a bit, he decided, and found himself on the coast road heading back towards Frantham. He drove past the turn off for the town and out towards the half-dozen houses where Ted Eebry lived and pulled over on to the grass verge a few hundred yards shy of the crescent.

For several minutes Andy sat undecided, fingers tapping at the steering wheel and his mind on the conversation he'd had with Miriam and with Kath's old friends. It had sort of clarified things but also added to his unease. Finally he got out and took a well-remembered path across the fields to where the gardens backed on to the farmland.

The wildlife pond was still there, scummy and over-grown now and not as big or as deep as he remembered it, though it *had* been a dry summer, he supposed. He wondered if any of the local kids played here now, came dipping with their nets and those funny little jars with the magnifying glasses on the top they all seemed to have back then.

Thinking about it, he seemed to remember Ted being the one that had brought them to the pond. Funny how the mind played tricks and memories faded into the background, only to return with almost vicious intensity. He'd not given much thought to the Eebry family in years—apart from his regular online conversations with Gail, that was—but now memories of Ted and the girls had come flooding back; it seemed they had permeated his childhood and teenage years without him knowing it or appreciating their significance.

He wished he'd called all this to mind before and not had these memories thrust upon him under such lousy circumstances.

Andy pushed through nettles that seemed set on world domination, and past the brambles, competing for the same honour and loaded with black fruit that stained his hands purple when he pushed them aside. He should have brought a bag, like he used to when he gathered blackberries for his mum. Moments later he was standing at the far end of Ted Eebry's garden and asking himself what the hell he was doing here.

From the back, Ted's house looked flat and very ordinary, but the garden was anything but. Close to the house it was all flowers and a lawn the girls had played on. There'd been a swing and climbing frame for a while. A paddling pool on hot days. Then a trellis screen covered with roses and clematis that divided the garden and a second screen that hid a bank of three compost bins and the potting shed. Andy could remember Ted's regime of turning and aerating until he'd produced a soft and good-smelling loam.

Two small greenhouses sat either side of the path and then a bit of a rock garden, a low hedge and then what Ted called his allotment. His kitchen garden, regimented and fruitful and, Andy could see now, planned with the greatest care: tall rows of beans, lower canes supporting peas, the fruit cage that protected the raspberries from the predations of birds. Another little potting shed and a compost heap close to the boundary where the newts were reputed to live and which was often overgrown with grass and weeds in summer. The one untidy spot in this entire large and lovely space.

Andy stared at the offending pile of leaves and vegetation slowly converting back into friable earth. There was no sign of a disturbance or use. Brambles from the field boundary had begun a slow incursion, as had the nettles, standing shoulder high atop the mound, but there was no sign of burial or exhumation.

Andy felt momentary relief and then reminded himself that the theory was that the bones had been moved long before now. After the flesh had rotted away, they had been moved and preserved before eventually some had been dumped at the dig site.

Or was he getting this completely wrong?

Keeping out of the sightline of the house, an easy task in such a fertile, blowsy location, Andy crossed to the second little potting shed and went inside. It was all very familiar. The scent of compost and stored onions, the bench under the windows with seed trays stacked beneath and different grades of garden riddle hanging from the hooks on the rear wall.

Andy leaned against the bench and stared at them. Five in all, two very old and rusty, the others newer but still showing signs of long use. He could remember Ted using them, getting just the right fineness for his pots and trays, sifting out the remaining roots and the odd stone from his homemade compost.

Andy turned away and let himself out, wanting to believe that everything would be all right now. Nothing was amiss and there was nothing left to find.

Then something caught his eye as he pushed back through the undergrowth close beside the boundary hedge. Andy bent and picked it up. It was small, palm-sized, and rusted almost through. Very fragile, but Andy knew it was part of another soil riddle from Ted's garden.

He searched his pockets for something he could put the object into and in the end had to make do with a couple of tissues wrapped carefully around the jagged wire.

He just knew it would be a match.

Andy remained crouched on the ground, breathing deep the scent of warm earth and blackberries and listening to the sound of bees and buzzing, and was in half a mind to leave the object where it lay. To let all this go.

Slowly, Andy got to his feet and, tissue-wrapped evidence held gingerly in his hand, walked back to his car.

THIRTY-TWO

George hadn't said much on the way home, and once they'd got out of the minibus he'd gone straight to his room. Ursula was due to help in the kitchen, getting dinner ready. All the kids took a turn with helping out; Cheryl said it was good for them. Ursula knew it wasn't just about the cooking; it was a chance for a private chat with one or other of their carers and key workers without it seeming odd or attracting attention from the other kids. She wondered if Mac had already contacted Hill House, but apparently he had not. Cheryl didn't say anything. She asked what sort of day they'd had and how Ursula was coping with the workload, and then the twins appeared and asked how long until dinner and she got distracted.

Ursula managed to respond in ways she knew Cheryl would find appropriate. Cheryl was proud that 'her' kids were doing well at school. Ursula knew the statistics: kids in care mostly left without much in the way of exam results. Her smile when Ursula told her she was coping OK, and thought George was too, was genuine.

'And are you feeling OK?' Cheryl asked, and Ursula knew she was talking about her dad.

She nodded, and then shook her head. 'Not really, but I guess it would be a bit weird if I was,' she said.

Cheryl nodded sympathetically and Ursula knew she'd said the right thing. And it was the truth. She didn't really know how she felt.

George was quiet at dinner too, but then he rarely said much anyway. The twins were down to help out with the washing up so Ursula and George took their homework and retreated to the conservatory.

'Do you think we should tell Cheryl?'

George shrugged. 'Tell her what?' He sounded so weary. She sat down next to him and took his hand. 'I just want to be left alone,' he said. 'I just want . . .'

'Yeah, I know.' Ursula didn't know what else to say.

'Maybe I should just run away, you know. I could do it. I've had enough bloody practice.'

'Only if I can come with you.'

'Yeah.'

They sat in silence, looking out at the dusk. The sky out at sea was bruised and black and heavy. Maybe there'd be a storm. The view from his window was fantastic when there was a storm out at sea. He could sit on his bed and watch the lightning, feel the chill as the rain lashed against his window and still be warm in bed. Still know that he wouldn't suddenly be woken in the night and have to run out into the rain with whatever they could grab, scared for their lives.

'No,' he said. 'We stop here and we face up to what comes. Whatever it is.'

He felt her nod and for a while they sat in silence, looking out at the changing sky.

'Do you think I might be like him?' she asked.

George knew she meant her dad.

'I get scared sometimes, when I feel down and everything gets too much, that I might be like him. That I might end up in a place like that. I'm scared of that, George.'

'You think I don't worry about that sort of stuff?' George demanded. 'My mum killed herself. My dad was a violent bastard and my sister is a complete psycho.'

'Yeah, but she loves you,' Ursula protested. She giggled awkwardly.

'And I love her too,' George admitted, 'and I miss her like you wouldn't believe, but I can't be like her or live like her or do like she wants me to do any more. I told her that. I've got to be me and you've just got to be you and if other people don't like it, well, fuck them all.'

'Fuck them all,' Ursula agreed.

George laughed. 'Sounds silly when you swear,' he said. 'You sound too posh.' He paused. Leaned in close to Ursula. The two of them rarely kissed, rarely did anything really intimate, and George knew they were the butt of a lot of jokes and innuendo because few people could figure out their relationship. He and Ursula understood one another though. They were neither of them ready for anything more just yet. George was only just getting used to being able to touch someone or be touched without feeling scared.

Before Ursula, there had only been Karen when it came to hugs or any kind of physical comfort. He'd always felt at ease with her.

He missed his sister so much it hurt, but he knew he couldn't have her back, not if he wanted to keep the new stuff that he'd gained.

'We've just got to let them go, don't we?'

Ursula nodded. 'I can't go and see him again. I just can't. I've not lived with him since I was five years old. I hardly know him. No one tells my mum she's got to go back to him. She's free to go off somewhere with someone else and everyone just says it's because she couldn't cope with it, like it's OK. But me, I'm his daughter and everyone wants—'

'Screw what they want. We've got to do what we want.' He laughed awkwardly. 'And you know what I want just now? I want to get my grades and maybe go to college and . . . and then I don't know.'

'How square are *you*?' It was a Cheryl phrase.

'No one says square.'

'Cheryl does.' Ursula laughed again and this time it was a real, honest, humorous sound.

George clasped her hand tight, glad she was there, and wishing Karen well, wherever she was, yet at the same time hoping she'd stay well out of the way.

THIRTY-THREE

Jerry had taken a big risk and called his handler again, slipping away for a few minutes when the others were ordering drinks in the hotel bar.

Calling from his room was out of the question. Haines picked up the tab for all of the accommodation and checked the phone calls assiduously. His mobile phone was billed direct to one of Haines's shell corporations—Jerry was on the payroll as a security consultant—and an unusual number, one not on Haines's approved list, would automatically be looked into; Haines employed people solely for that task. He'd risked keeping a cheap backup phone for a while, but Haines was given to ordering lightning searches, which he personally attended. He'd had a man thrown overboard for making unauthorized calls, or so Jerry had been told, and the use of public phones was on Haines's list of forbidden things.

It was, as someone had once commented, well out of his hearing, like living with the KGB.

Jerry was of the opinion that they might actually have been more forgiving.

The only time in recent history that he'd been free of such restrictions had been those few days in France. So why had he come back?

He'd come back because Haines would move heaven and earth to find him had he not. Jerry had thought about faking his own death, but that took resources he couldn't assemble in a hurry, and besides, there were others at risk should he betray his master.

Haines had a way of finding out whom and what you cared about. Haines knew he was an ex-copper, apparently thrown out on his ear for misappropriation of certain substances that should have remained in the evidence locker. He employed Jerry in part because of the connections he still had, and as for the rest, well, just because he had divorced his wife—or, to be precise, she had divorced him—it didn't mean he wanted her dead.

Most people, in Jerry's experience, had someone they'd rather remain alive and intact. There were few exceptions. Santos, maybe. Jerry couldn't think of anyone Santos cared about.

Checking that the others were engrossed in conversation, he headed off towards the gents, then swung right and crossed the lobby to a small office he had spotted a few days earlier and which seemed to be unoccupied for much of the day. He hoped it had an outside line. He closed the door until just a crack remained and grabbed the cordless phone. His relief when he got a dial tone was overwhelming. He dialled fast, got through. 'You got my message?'

'I got it. What the hell are you playing at?'

'Trying to stay alive.'

'Jerry, listen to me, I can't do anything for you yet. Things are moving fast. We've got new intel—'

'I don't give a damn. Look, you've got to get me out now. We're leaving tomorrow, going back to that blasted boat of his. It's now or—'

'Hang in there. Just a few more days. A couple of weeks at most.'

Jerry had heard that so many times before.

'Fuck you,' Jerry said. 'Fuck the lot of you.'

He hung up and stared at the phone as though he could lay the blame there. He was on his own, he knew it now. On his own.

He replaced the phone and returned to the bar, claimed his drink.

'Where did you get to?' Santos said. 'We were about to send out a search party.'

Tomas laughed and handed Jerry his drink.

He was on his own now, Jerry knew that for certain. They'd just abandoned him, hung him out to dry. He raised his glass in a mock toast. 'Old friends,' he said, aware that Santos was watching him.

* * *

'He's losing his nerve and frankly I can't say I blame him.'

'You think he'll blow his cover?'

'No, never that. He knows what that would mean. I've told him two more weeks at most and this time we have to mean that. I'm not standing aside and watching more broken promises. We should have pulled him out long before this.'

'He knew what the risks were.'

'Risks for six months, not three years.'

'Oh, come off it, the effort we'd put into creating his legend, he knew it would be for longer than that. The man isn't a complete fool.'

'Isn't he? He said yes to us, didn't he?' Didcott stubbed out his cigarette. 'If you want him to be alive long enough to testify then we need to give him a way out and we need to do it fast, before he takes matters into his own hands, whatever the risk. You can only use people for so long before they rebel and, believe me, Jerry is on the verge of that rebellion.'

THIRTY-FOUR

It was late when Karen phoned Peverill Lodge. The household had retired to bed, all except Stan, who was still having trouble getting up the stairs. It took him a while to reach the phone, but he got there on the eighth ring.

'Ah,' Karen said. 'Mr Holden.'

'Miss Parker. Or is it Miss Munroe?'

'Whatever. Has Rina gone to bed? She sent me a message.'

'You want me to get her?' His heart sank at the thought of struggling up the stairs.

'No. I think you might do. Now what's been happening, Stan the man? I hear you've been having a spot of bother.'

Stan made his way back to the living room and eased himself on to the sofa. He told her what had occurred with Haines and what threats he had made. 'Mac said he'd take care of George,' he said.

'Oh, Mac is it now? You friends with a policeman, Stan? That's a bit of a turn up, isn't it?'

Stan didn't rise to the bait. 'So what should we do?' he said.

'Well, if you want me to come over so you can take a shot at satisfying Haines, I think I'll have to decline.'

'Girl, right now you could lie on the floor and put a gun to your own head and I don't think I could reach over to pull the trigger.'

'Haines did a good job, then.'

'Well, Jerry Mason and Santos did, which amounts to the same thing. But as Rina observed rather tartly, I'm still alive, so . . .'

Karen laughed. 'Look,' she said. 'I need to think on this one, but I will sort it. Oh, and one more thing, you can tell your new policeman friend that I did for Brig Morten. I expect they'll have a suspect list a mile long and they're bound to jump to the wrong conclusion, so just to keep things straight.'

'Brig who?'

'Ah, it'll be on the news in the morning. Surprised it hasn't been already, but I suppose they want to be sure of the proper identification. I did leave rather a mess.'

'I'll pass your message on,' Stan said, feeling the moment was more than a little surreal. 'You'll be in touch, then? Once you've decided what to do?'

'Maybe. Maybe I won't have to. I've about finished here, I think.'

'And you're leaving for good, then?'

She laughed again. 'Tell Rina not to worry. I'm not planning on sticking around. Brig Morten was the last thing on my list. Haines has complicated things a bit, of course, but I'm not planning on expending too much energy in that direction. I really don't have time. Clean break and all that. Time to be someone else now.'

The phone went dead and when Stan dialled 1471 he was unsurprised to find the number was withheld. What did Karen have in mind? he wondered. He settled down to sleep, more than satisfied that she would keep her word and deal with it, and trying not to think too much about how.

THIRTY-FIVE

Stan's call to Mac had been made first thing in the morning
on Wednesday, Rina having provided his mobile number.
He arrived post-breakfast, accepting tea and toast as compen-
sation for having missed the full English, and joined Stan and
Rina in the large living room.

Stan, he thought, still looked like hell.

'Karen phoned me last night,' Stan said. 'She said not to
worry about Haines, she'd sort it, and also that she'd killed
someone called Brig Morten, just so you know.'

Mac almost choked on his tea. 'She said what?'

'Um, up north somewhere. Big fella, it was on the news
this morning. Looks like she shot him.'

Mac stared at him. He had seen the news, noted the
murder investigation, thought little more about it. 'She said
she did it? Did she say why? Do you believe her?'

'I don't see why not. Karen seemed to be quite sanguine
about it. In fact she sounded positively cheerful. And I didn't
feel it was appropriate to ask for an explanation.'

'Right,' Mac said. 'And what else did she say?'

'Not a great deal. She said she was leaving. That this
Brig Morten was the last thing on her list, until Haines

complicated things, but she was planning on going away. For good, she said.'

'Which would be a relief to a great many of us,' Rina said tartly. 'Mac, I spoke to the solicitor on Monday. As far as I can tell the trust is all set up legitimately. I don't want to guess where the money came from, but the solicitors are satisfied that it is in fact a legacy.' She explained briefly what she had been told and showed the paperwork to Mac.

'How has she swung this?'

'I've no idea, but on the Canadian side they employed a forensic accountant to check things out and the money comes up clean. I've agreed to be executor and signed the papers.'

'Rina, you did what? You realize that could make you an accessory?'

'Mac, it all checks out. There is no evidence to say that Karen Munroe is really Karen Parker. There is apparently no evidence that this money she has put in trust is profit from crime. I won't deprive George of the future she has secured for him.'

'Rina.' Mac gave up and closed his eyes. 'What if it all crashes around his ears? Or yours?'

'Then we face that problem if it arises. I think there are more immediate issues and concerns, don't you? And Mac, I'm not planning on telling you any more about this. I know you disapprove. I've noted that. You'll pardon me if I do what I feel is the right thing here.'

'I have to look into this. You know that?'

'Then you too must do what you think is right. Karen's solicitors have instigated major investigations of their own and come up with nothing. I'm sure you will get the same result.'

Mac got up and prepared to leave. 'Rina, I don't like you being involved in this.'

'Mac, I've been involved since we first met. Since I first made friends with young George. I can't not be involved.'

* * *

Andy spent time comparing the wire grid he had found to the marks on the bone. Miriam had explained how to match the scale of the photograph to actual size and how to print and then overlay the fragment of mesh. There could be no doubt, Andy realized. It was a match. Much as he looked and retraced and sought to analyse the evidence away, it wouldn't go. The pattern on the wire mesh exactly matched the criss-cross tracing on the bone.

Andy's suspicions had crystallized, and he did not like the conclusion he had reached. He didn't want to know. He felt the need to seek some advice, some reassurance even, so he went to the little café on the promenade and brought a caffeine- and vanilla-laced offering back to Frank Baker.

Sergeant Baker accepted it with due grace. 'What's on your mind, boy?'

'I think those bones belong to Kath Eebry,' Andy said. 'Frank, I don't know what to do.'

Frank sipped his coffee and studied his young under-study thoughtfully. 'Sit yourself down and tell me about it,' he said. 'What evidence do we have?'

What indeed? Andy sighed. 'It's all circumstantial,' he said. 'It's little things and it's feelings and it's . . . Oh, I don't know. Look, let me run it by you and tell me what you think.'

As coherently as he could, Andy explained his reasoning and presented his meagre evidence. The mesh that may have left the marks on the bones. The mystery of Kath Eebry's disappearance and Ted's sudden insistence that she had left to be with another man. The awkwardness he sensed in the older man that he could not explain.

He listed it all and was shocked and somewhat relieved at how flimsy it all sounded.

Frank listened. 'Drink your coffee, boy. Now let's have a think about this, shall we.'

Andy sat in silence while Frank thought. 'Well?' he said at last.

'I think you may be right,' Frank said. 'I think you have little enough to make a case—not enough for the CPS to take it forward is my guess. No, now don't think you're off the hook,' he added as Andy began to look visibly relieved. 'What you have to think next is what you plan to do.'

'That's just it,' Andy said miserably. 'I don't know what to do. This is Ted Eebry. I've known him almost all my life. I played in his garden, I ate beans on toast at his table, I'm friends with his daughters.'

'So you should hand what you have over to someone else and take yourself off the case. Personal involvement, Andy, that's not permitted, you know.'

Andy nodded. 'But if I do that, then someone else will have to go and talk to Ted. Someone else will . . . Unless you think there really isn't enough evidence?'

Frank Baker patted him on the arm. 'Andy, the rules are there for a reason. They're there to protect people from pain like this. Look, lad, you've done a good job. You shouldn't, by rights, have been left with the burden of this. Bring your notes up to date and I'll see the boss takes it over.'

Andy nodded. 'I might have it completely wrong,' he said. 'I might have listened to too much gossip.'

'Or you might just have made use of local knowledge. Andy, there's often a very fine line between the two.'

Andy nodded, knowing that Frank Baker was right. But that it didn't help. He'd started this and he'd have to see it through.

THIRTY-SIX

They would be leaving within the hour and Jerry knew he would have to take this opportunity or it would be gone. Once back on board the ironically named *Spirit of Unity* he would have no chance. Santos had been watching him more closely, Jerry was sure of that, and Tomas had taken to appearing suddenly whenever Jerry chanced to be alone.

Jerry packed and brought his bags down, together with his camera bag and backpack. He dumped them on the trolley with the rest, ensuring that the camera bag was strapped to one of the heavier bits of luggage as he always did.

He could see Santos watching him, Tomas standing on the other side of the lobby studying them both. Jerry turned and went back to the bank of lifts at the rear of the lobby. He could feel Santos's eyes upon him as he pressed the call button for his floor. He stepped inside, praying Santos wouldn't follow, or if he did that the doors would close before he reached them. The doors slid closed and Jerry breathed deeply. He caught sight of himself in the pink toned mirror of the lift interior: close-cut hair, hard, grey eyes. Tired. He looked appallingly tired. He should have taken the opportunity when in France to simply melt away, and he would have done had it not been for Louise.

After the divorce she had gone away. Jerry hadn't known where. He'd risked a call to her parents, but they wouldn't even speak with him, never mind provide a forwarding address. But Haines had known, as Haines always did, and now, at last, Jerry did too; months of careful, fearful searching through Haines's files had finally provided him with that last, essential element. And that was the missing piece of his plan. Not that there was much of a plan; Jerry was now just riding his luck.

On the third floor the lift halted and a couple got in. Jerry seized his chance and got out. Moments later he was on the back stairs, heading down and praying that his luck would hold and Santos not anticipate what he had done. The stairs led to the kitchens and the utility areas at the rear of the hotel. Jerry knew that much, but beyond that he would have to guess. He slowed his pace on the final flight, listening, risking a glance over the rail and down to the passageway below. So far as he could see there was no one there. Almost not daring to breathe, he rushed down the last steps and paused.

Sounds from his right told him the kitchens were that way. To be avoided if possible. A door to the left declared itself to be the laundry room, another proved to be just a store cupboard. So right it would have to be.

Cautiously, he started along the corridor, listening for anything that didn't sound like the crash of pots and pans. How long had he been gone? Santos would have seen the couple come down. Would it dawn on him that the lift had not risen to the fifth floor before it returned?

Of course it bloody would. Jerry would have noticed so it was certain Santos would.

This was beyond caution, Jerry thought. This was beyond going back, too.

He could see the door to the kitchen further along the passageway, and through that the door that led to the dining room and from there to the bar and the lobby and the front of the hotel. Surely there had to be another way, or did he have to risk the kitchen? And then he saw it: a little recess he'd taken for a door to another store cupboard, but which he saw now was an emergency exit.

Would it set off an alarm?

Almost certainly, Jerry thought, but he'd have to risk it. Glancing back towards the stairs he thought he heard a sound, a tiny scrape as though metal caught against the banister.

Jerry knew he couldn't wait. He made a leap for the recessed door and pushed the bar, praying it wasn't the kind with the magnetic lock that released only if the fire alarm sounded.

It gave beneath his hands, the door flew open and Jerry ran, suddenly aware that there had been someone on the stairs and that it had been Santos and that now he was giving chase; instinct told Jerry that Tomas would not be far behind.

Jerry ran out from behind the hotel and into the busy street lined with shops and cafés. Would they risk shooting at him? Jerry jinked right and left between the shoppers, Santos in hot pursuit. Where was Tomas? He'd be somewhere close, Jerry knew that. He knew how Haines's people operated. He'd been one of them for long enough, hadn't he?

Abruptly, he changed direction, striking out across the busy road, until he spotted Tomas, running parallel and now on the opposite pavement and heading him off.

'Shit.' Jerry's lungs burned. He was fit and fast but fear and adrenalin tightened his airways and made his limbs feel like lead. He spun around and headed back the way he had come, catching Santos off guard but only for a split second. They were both on his heels now and Jerry could hear the shouts and yells of shoppers who found themselves in the way.

And then he spotted his chance, only a slim chance but it was there. A man had pulled up at the side of the road to let his passenger out. He seemed unaware of the panic on the street.

Jerry launched himself at the car, tugging at the door. The man turned in panic, yelped in fear that was nothing compared to the terror Jerry was now feeling.

'Out. Get the fuck out.'

The man fumbled with his seat belt and Jerry could almost feel Santos's breath on his back. He pulled the man out of the car and on to the road. The shoppers had seen him now and someone shouted in protest. The passenger was screaming on the pavement. A police officer ran from the opposite side of the road and Santos swerved away as he spotted him.

Jerry slammed the door shut and gunned the engine, taking off in first and redlining before he managed to shift the gears. The driver had been shorter and the seat too close to the wheel and pedals for Jerry's long legs. Jerry hurtled down the road, narrowly avoiding the line of cars stopping at the lights. Behind him was mayhem. This was not the discreet exit Jerry had been hoping for. He wondered just how many of the crowd would have captured events on their mobile phones, and how many CCTV pictures there would be of his dramatic escape.

You've done it now, Jerry. Boy have you done it now.

At the end of the road he went with the flow and turned left. No way was he going to be able to use this as a getaway car. But he had to get away from the bloody CCTV cameras before he could do anything more. First chance he got, he swung the car down a side road and then into another, finally pulling into the drive of a semi-detached house. He got out and looked back down the road. No one there, just the slow flow of normal traffic and a single dog walker.

Jerry crossed the road, knowing that time was very much against him. He began to walk, looking for a way to get off the street. He cut down a passageway between a house and a shop, found it led only to a back garden, but at least he was off the road and out of sight. He paused to take stock. He needed a car, but first he needed to put more distance between himself and the hotel. Closing his eyes, he visualized the route he had just taken, working out where he was in relation to Haines and the rest. The sound of a police siren jolted him back to the here and now. He listened as it became louder and then faded again, obviously heading towards the chaos he had created on the main road. A moment later he heard a second siren, then a third.

At least, Jerry thought, that might make Haines think twice about sending out his men. Santos and Tomas, like Jerry, would have been seen, could be identified. Haines would recall them and keep them close. With luck . . .

Cautiously, Jerry left the shelter of the little alleyway, checking no one saw him as he stepped back on to the street and walked away.

THIRTY-SEVEN

Today it was Karen who was waiting when George and Ursula got out of school. George was dumbfounded.

'What the hell are you doing here?'

'Well, hello to you too, little brother. Don't worry, I won't be stopping, I just need you to get this to Mac. Bit of luck and it'll sort out Haines and a bit more besides.' She held out a large Manila envelope.

'What is it?' George demanded.

'Just some papers. It won't bite. Just take it to Mac for me.'

It was Ursula who reached out and took it from her. 'Are you leaving for good now?'

Karen smiled at her, but unusually for Karen it was a genuine smile with no sense of threat in it. 'I'm leaving, yes.'

'For good?' George sounded uncertain now. 'Will I see you again?'

'Maybe. One day. I'll send postcards. George, you'll be OK. Oh, and Rina should be in touch soon, she's got some news for you that I hope will make everything a bit easier.'

'What news?'

'Oh, she'll explain. Goodbye, kiddo. I love you, don't forget that.'

George nodded. His fists were clenched and his face white beneath the freckles. He watched as his sister turned and walked away. Watched until he was certain she would not look back. His shoulders sagged and he tried hard not to cry.

Ursula reached out and took his hand. 'Come on,' she said, 'or we'll be keeping the minibus waiting again.'

* * *

Kendall had managed to supply an officer to look out for George between school and bus. He wasn't convinced there was a need, but Mac had pricked his conscience. When Karen had approached, DC Colin Brady had watched, wondering if he should intervene. He didn't know who the dark-haired young woman was, only that the kids seemed to know her and the boy seemed upset.

He watched the handover of the envelope with interest, wondering what it meant, and then took pictures of all three participants with his mobile phone and sent them to Kendall. Finally he began to tail the two teenagers to the bus stop.

The woman's voice was soft and educated. Something made him notice that. What he noticed more was the something she had pressed against his back.

'And you are?' Karen said.

'DC Brady. I'm DC Brady.'

'And what are you doing here?'

'I'm watching George Parker. Keeping an eye.' Brady could hear the shake in his voice and he was ashamed of it. What the hell was she going to do?

'Alone, DC Brady?'

He nodded.

'Then you'd best go and do your job. Don't turn around, DC Brady. I'll know if you do.'

Brady froze. Whatever it was had gone from the middle of his back. He swallowed hard, wondering if he dared to turn around.

'Well, go on then,' Karen said. 'They're getting way ahead of you.'

Stiff-legged, Brady walked on. When he did dare to look around he saw only an empty street. He was torn between chasing after the girl and watching over the kids, and furious with himself for being such a wuss. Not sure what else to do, he followed George and called DI Kendall.

'I'm guessing you just met Karen Parker,' Kendall told him. 'Think yourself lucky, Col. The last two men to get that close to her ended up dead.'

THIRTY-EIGHT

Andy drove past Ted's house. Ted's car wasn't there and he felt slightly relieved. He had to act, but not just yet. That morning he'd followed Frank Baker's advice and handed everything over to Mac, but he still couldn't rest easy. He noticed that the For Sale sign had been taken down. So Ted was no longer planning to move. That was a sudden decision. In a way it just reinforced Andy's suspicions: the rest of Kath Eebry's bones must still be at the house. The publicity and excitement must have made it impossible for him to dispose of them and so now he'd decided that he dare not move.

Andy hated his job at that moment, but he also knew in that instant what he had to do. Ted Eebry had been his friend.

* * *

What to do with the envelope Karen had given him? So many things went through George's mind on the trip home, but it seemed that Ursula had decided for them. She had texted Mac and said they needed to see him. Now, tonight, but not at Hill House. By the time they reached home, it was arranged. They would meet DI MacGregor on the cliff path in half an hour. They dumped their bags and went back outside, slipping across the lawn on to the public footpath and heading towards Frantham and the De Barr hotel.

Mac arrived about ten minutes after they did.

'We can't stop,' Ursula said. 'Cheryl is a stickler for meal times, you know.'

'I know,' Mac agreed. He took the envelope from them. 'Have you opened this?'

'No, we thought best not to. We just wanted it gone.'

'How are you both?' Mac asked. 'I'm sorry for lately . . . I've been clumsy. I'm sorry.'

'We're OK,' George said. 'Don't worry about it. We'll be all right. Right, better go.'

Mac watched as they walked away, wondering if he should offer to go with them, anxious that they should not be out alone, despite the fact it was only a ten-minute walk back to Hill House and he could see from where he stood that the path was empty even of other walkers. He watched them anyway, and it was only as they left the path and returned to the gardens of Hill House that he turned back towards his car.

* * *

Only a few miles from where they stood on the cliff top, Haines was preparing to board his yacht. He was in a fine fury. Karen Parker was now far from his mind; the new target of his rage was Jerry Mason.

Santos and Tomas were ready to leave. The address of Louise Mason, Jerry's ex-wife, was in their hands, as were instructions to deal with both her and Jerry. And they were to do it any way they liked; Haines didn't care.

Santos was relishing the idea.

Haines warned them: 'Don't come back with the job half done.'

THIRTY-NINE

Mac had been about to call DI Kendall when his phone rang and Kendall saved him the bother. Mac found himself being summoned to Dorchester and an hour later was sitting in a hastily assembled incident room in the bar of a rather smart hotel.

'Jerry Mason,' Kendall said when he met Mac in the lobby.

'Your undercover man.'

'Not any more. He made a rather dramatic exit about three o'clock this afternoon. Oh, and your Karen was spotted meeting her brother out of school. I put a man on point, Karen spotted him. I sent him home to change his pants.'

'She's not my Karen,' Mac said. 'And I know.'

Kendall looked at the package he held. 'Ah,' he said. 'The envelope. My man sent me pictures. What's in it?'

'That,' Mac said, 'is a good question, but Karen seemed to think it would be effective against Haines.'

Kendall sniffed. 'Doesn't smell like garlic,' he said. 'Right, come on through and I'll introduce you.'

There were nine people present in the little conference room. Mac didn't catch all their names, but one of them was called Didcott and it seemed he had been responsible for

Jerry. It was also obvious that he was hopping mad, though Mac was not immediately sure if it was with Jerry or with another man who, Mac gathered, had been responsible for not agreeing to a more dignified exit from Haines's crew.

They showed him pictures of Jerry's precipitate escape captured from CCTV.

'Mobile phone footage is already making it on to YouTube,' Kendall said, 'and the local media will lap up everything else.'

They also had pictures of Karen talking to Ursula and George. Mac laid the contents of the envelope on the table. The man called Didcott shuffled through the pages. He stopped at one that showed a list of figures; one group had been circled.

'You did this?' he asked of Mac.

'No. Karen must have done. It's the same set of numbers as were on the slip of paper Jerry gave to Stan Holden and I gave to Kendall.'

From the glances cast around the table, Mac gathered that not everyone was au fait with the Stan Holden connection. He decided he would leave that for Kendall to explain.

'You have no idea where she got this from?' Didcott asked.

Mac shook his head. 'I think she believes it will bring Haines down and that will protect her brother. That's all I know.'

'And that's assumption,' someone else commented.

Mac shrugged. 'Is it a correct assumption?'

'Oh yes,' Didcott approved. 'And taken with Jerry Mason's testimony it will do a great deal more. So we'd better make bloody sure Jerry survives to testify.'

'How do we know he will? If he's gone rogue . . .'

'If he had he'd have stayed with Haines,' Didcott said irritably. 'He ran because he'd reached his limits, most likely because he knew his cover was compromised. He'd reached out to us three times and each time we let him down. What the hell else was he supposed to do?'

'Does he have family?' Mac asked quietly. 'It's the way Haines keeps his people in line. His ultimate sanction.'

'Very poetic,' Didcott said. 'His parents are dead, no siblings or close family, but he does have an ex-wife. She divorced him and we lost track of her. I believe Jerry did too.'

'Haines will know where she is,' Mac said.

FORTY

Somehow, Jerry had believed there would be more time. That he'd be able to call Louise and warn her and she would listen to him and get away somewhere before the danger could get to her.

But here, the luck that had stayed with him for the rest of the day seemed to have run dry. The phone rang and there was no answer. Louise was not home so she could not be warned.

Three times he tried and three times the phone rang out into empty space. In desperation he tried her parents' old number but someone else answered the phone.

They had moved a year ago and no, the new tenant did not know where, and why should he tell Jerry if he did?

'Who are you?' the man asked, worried by Jerry's tone and his insistence. 'Who the hell are you?'

Jerry had hung up. What to do, what to do?

He thought of calling Didcott, but didn't know if he could trust the man to help after all the recent failures to assist him. He needed help, someone who could get through to Louise before Haines's men arrived.

He could steal another car, drive up there, hope to stay ahead of them.

No, too risky. Haines had resources. Fast cars, probably men close to where Louise lived that he could call upon. Jerry had already wasted too much time. In the end he could think of only one place to go for help, and he wasn't even sure where that was, only that it was somewhere in Frantham.

He found himself another vehicle and drove along the coast road to the little seaside town, wasted even more time looking for a particular house, the street or the number of which he didn't know, only that Haines had referred to it once as something Lodge. He knew it was Victorian, but so was half the town. In the end persistence paid off and he found himself in Newell Street facing Peverill Lodge and was sure then he had heard that name before. This was where Stan Holden was holed up.

It was late and the lights were out, but he knocked on the door anyway, glancing side to side along the deserted street.

Someone open the bloody door!

Slow footsteps told him someone had heard and the light went on in the hall. The door opened a crack and Jerry pushed it all the way, knocking Stan almost off his feet.

'What the fuck are you doing here?'

'You look a bloody mess.'

'Thanks to you and frigging Santos.' Stan looked past him suspiciously, as though Santos might be waiting outside.

Wearily, Jerry shoved the door closed. 'I don't want trouble. I just need your help.'

'And why the hell should I help you?'

* * *

From the landing Rina listened to the angry voices coming from the hall. Stan sounded pained and distressed and the other voice was not a familiar one.

Oh, Stan, don't you know about putting the chain on the door? That's what it's there for.

She tightened the belt of her dressing gown and crept softly down the stairs on slippered feet, her husband's old

212

cricket bat clasped tightly in her hand. The voices had moved from hall to dining room now and the stranger's voice sounded all the more insistent and strained. Who was he?

Rina crept across the hall, careful to keep out of sight of the door, moving forward soft and fast. Stan stood a little way into the room and the stranger just inside the doorway, his back to her. Rina didn't hesitate: the bat came down across his shoulders and head and Jerry Mason was felled.

'Rina! What the hell are you doing?' Stan bent over the injured man.

'I thought you were in trouble. Who on earth is he?'

'His name is Jerry Mason. He came here looking for help.'

'Oh.' Rina parked the bat against the door and helped Stan lift her dazed victim to his feet and then into a chair. 'You're the undercover policeman,' she said. 'Oh, don't fuss, Stan, I didn't hit him that hard. I wasn't really trying.'

Jerry held his head in his hands and then tried to look at Rina. 'They'll be going after Louise,' he said. 'Haines will have sent them by now, and she won't answer her phone.'

'You'd best call Mac,' Stan said. 'Tell him to get over here. We can't handle this one on our own.'

FORTY-ONE

'We've got an address for the ex-wife,' Mac said. 'I've got Jerry Mason here and he's sure Haines will have sent men after her by now. He can't raise her by phone so it's possible she's away.'

He dictated the address to Kendall. 'Get the locals involved, but tell them they'll need an armed response unit.'

'Jerry Mason's with you? Where the hell are you anyway?'

Mac told him. 'And you'd best send an ambulance while you're at it. Rina crowned him with a cricket bat. He's a little concussed.'

'I apologized,' Rina said. 'Mac, will it be all right now? There shouldn't be more bloodshed.'

'Kendall will take care of it,' he said. He sat down wearily at Rina's kitchen table. Eliza's first aid skills had been called into play once again, but Jerry still looked sick and Mac felt he should be somewhere with a proper medic.

'I should be there,' Jerry objected.

'You can drive that fast? Jerry, even without a concussion it would take the best part of three hours. Time to let someone else take responsibility. She'll be OK. Kendall will ring me as soon as there's anything to tell.'

* * *

A few miles distant, events had been set in motion on several fronts. Didcott had taken control and somehow everything was moving that bit faster because of that. Warrants had been issued for Haines and Vaschinsky and the coastguard had been mobilized to aid in the arrests on *The Spirit of Unity*.

Local police were called upon to find Louise Mason and an armed response unit would be in position within the hour.

Didcott rubbed his hands in satisfaction. He now wanted to speak with Jerry Mason.

'He doesn't want to speak with you,' Kendall told him. 'He said that explicitly. Not until he knows Louise is safe. Besides, he's on his way to the local hospital. It seems Rina Martin mistook him for the enemy and wrapped a cricket bat round his ear.'

'Sir?' one of the sergeants called to Kendall. 'It's DI Barnes, he wants a word.'

Kendall nodded and went off to liaise with the armed response unit heading for Louise Mason's home.

* * *

After that it was pretty much a waiting game. Local officers were dispatched to protect Jerry Mason at the hospital, and Mac went to join the teams being organized by Didcott. Rina hoped he would be there to view Haines's arrest and, as she sat drinking tea with Stan and the other members of her little family, she could not help but feel a sense of anti-climax and regret that she could do no more.

FORTY-TWO

Louise Mason worked shifts at a local garage and convenience store. Technically, she was currently working the two 'til ten, but, as always, the place was short-staffed and she'd agreed to a couple of hours' overtime, so it was midnight before she could even consider getting away. At half past midnight, her manager finally arrived to relieve her. She had to find another bloody job, Louise thought. It was beyond a joke.

She was about to get into her car when a police patrol pulled on to the forecourt and someone got out and called her name.

'Mrs Mason?'

'Yes?'

'Mrs Mason, my name is DI Barnes. I need to have a word.'

* * *

Tomas James and Santos had arrived at Louise Mason's house just after ten and parked a few hundred yards down the road. They had gone around the back of the little house, a two up two down at the end of a row. A light was on in the kitchen, but it was soon evident there was no one home. Satisfied that they could return without being observed by nosy neighbours, they went back to their car and prepared to wait.

'You reckon Jerry will show?'

Santos shrugged. 'He'll show. He's still soft on her and he knows how the boss deals with disloyalty.' Santos laughed. 'I bloody hope he'll show. He makes us go looking for him and I'll not be best pleased.'

* * *

'I don't understand.' Louise shook her head vehemently. 'I've not seen my ex-husband for three years. This has nothing to do with me.'

Patiently, DI Barnes explained again that it did not matter. This was not a matter of logic. The threat was real.

'I told him it was the job or me,' Louise said. 'He chose . . . and now you're telling me . . .'

'Suspect car about a hundred yards down from your position. Can we get the neighbours out?'

'Next door have been evacuated. The neighbours in the next one down are on holiday. Do you have a visual on the car?'

'Two occupants matching the descriptions.'

A car drove slowly down past Santos and Tomas and parked outside Louise's house.

'They've spotted you. Get yourself inside and we'll move in.'

A female got out of Louise's car and walked up to the front door. Went inside.

'Wait until they start to move. Then on my mark . . .'

It took ten minutes before the two men in the car made their move. Then Santos got out, followed by Tomas, and the signal was given to move in.

'Armed Police! Get down on the floor! Get down on the floor! Hands where I can see them, get down on the floor!'

Officers surrounded them. Tomas James knelt beside the car. For a moment Santos stood, uncertain, then he lowered his hands, smiled at Tomas and went for his gun. Moments later he lay dead in the road, blood pooling, slick around his head.

* * *

'It's over,' Mac said. 'She's fine. And the coastguard are preparing to board Haines's boat. Didcott wants to see you now. Can I tell him yes?'

Jerry turned his face away, trying to regain some semblance of control. 'I'll talk to him,' he said. 'I'll see him now.'

FORTY-THREE

Ted was not surprised when Andy knocked on his door the next afternoon. He stood aside and let him come in and then led the way to the kitchen. Andy sat down at the table and Ted filled the kettle.

'Ted, I—'

Ted Eebry waved him into silence. 'Don't apologize. I knew this day would come, I suppose. I just wanted to see the girls grown up and settled. I couldn't bear . . . couldn't bear to think of them being dumped somewhere they weren't wanted. Missing me as well as their mam. Maybe even being separated. So I hid what had happened. I said I didn't know where Kath had gone.'

'Ted, I shouldn't be here. I shouldn't be doing this.'

'Well I'm glad it's you. Really I am. It's better to see a friendly face.'

'Stacey and Gail will hate me.' It was such a selfish thing to say, but he couldn't help himself.

'Not if I tell them not to. It's not your fault. Really it's not.'

'What happened, Ted? What happened to Kath?'

Ted Eebry filled the teapot and brought it to the table. He seemed very calm now. Andy was anything but.

'It was in the garden,' he said. 'May twelfth, sixteen years ago. She'd been out there with me helping in the allotment and that was something she never did. She wasn't a gardener, our Kath, but I knew she had something on her mind and she needed time to get it straight in her head before she could tell me. I spent the day thinking all manner of stuff, Andy, working myself up into a sweat over what might be nothing. And then, just as we were packing up for the day she told me. She'd had a bit of a fling with a man she'd met at work. It was nothing, over in a few weeks, and she felt badly about it, but she said she'd found it exciting and she said the excitement seemed to have gone out of our marriage lately. She had finished with him and I said it was alright. I forgave her. It didn't matter.'

'Didn't it, Ted? Didn't it really matter?'

He shrugged. 'Andy, I don't know. Yes it would have done, yes it might have been something that festered, but we'll never know, will we, because of what I did.'

'And what did you do, Ted?'

'The wrong thing. I said the wrong thing, didn't I? Kath didn't want to be forgiven, she wanted me to notice her, to feel angry and jealous and be . . . exciting, I suppose, the way that man at work had been. Andy, something I've understood since is that people want their moment. They see anger as cleansing, somehow, as what it takes to really make amends. If you don't get mad, it means you don't care. It wasn't that I didn't care, it was that I cared so much she could have done just about anything and I'd have forgiven and still loved her.'

'Would you?'

Ted shrugged. 'I don't know. What does anybody know?'

'So what happened, Ted?'

Ted Eebry poured their tea and offered Andy the milk.

'She flew at me, all fists and fury and words she knew would hurt because she wanted to be hurt herself. Wanted me to be angry so she could be forgiven properly. At least, that's what I think she wanted.'

He paused for a moment and looked at Andy as though trying to work out what *he* wanted to hear.

'So what did you do?' Andy felt oddly calm now.

'I pushed her away. I pushed her away and she fell. Hit her head on the edge of the spade we'd just left half stuck into the ground. She fell back and she hit her head on the corner of the blade and then she just lay still and that was it. My Kath was dead, and all I could think was that the kids would be home soon and they mustn't see her lying there like that.'

Andy wasn't sure how to proceed. 'Are you sure she was dead?' he asked gently. 'Are you certain?'

'I checked for a pulse. I tried to wake her up. I was so scared, Andy, I could only think that the kids mustn't see her.'

'You could have called the police. Called an ambulance. Ted, what did you do?'

'I buried her. In the garden. I took the top off the old compost heap and dug down inside as far as I could go, and once I'd got a hollow place underneath it I put her in, then I shovelled the muck back and I covered her over and I put the top layer back like it had been before, and then I came in and got things ready for the kids' teas.'

'Just like that?'

'Just like that.'

Andy stared at Ted, his brain whirring. 'And you left her there? We all played there. We all climbed and jumped and . . .' Andy felt sick.

'I didn't know what else to do. I took the kids out of school and we went off for the summer. The school was sympathetic, everyone was. I knew by the time we got back she'd be . . . Well, the worst of any smell would be gone, you know. I'd dug down deep before I put her under and things rot down fast in a big heap like that and we were gone from May right through to September.'

'This was your wife, Ted.'

'And they were my kids. I had to do it for them.'

Andy no longer knew what to think. 'Ted, why did you move the body?'

Ted sighed. 'It was a false alarm about five years ago,' he said. 'The water company said it was going to run a new main across behind the crescent and it looked on the plans like they'd be coming through the hedge, like. Through the heap. So I waited till the kids were away for the day, staying with friends. Not that Stacey was a kid by then of course, already a young woman, and she looked so much like my Kath. And I dug up what was left of her and I put the bones in an old tin box I'd got in the shed and I left her there. I left her in the box.'

Andy swallowed hard, wishing he'd done as he should and accompanied Mac, or Frank, or someone else, anyone really, so that he'd not been here alone.

'Ted, I think I need to call my boss. We need to get this down official like. A proper statement.'

Ted nodded. 'Then our Stacey wanted me to move and I had to think what to do. Then I saw the story about the old bones they found at the aerodrome, and I thought, why not put my Kath's bones there too? Hiding in plain sight, if you see what I mean. But I knew I'd have to kind of do a bit at a time.'

'You couldn't possibly have thought that would work, Ted.'

'I didn't think,' Ted said. 'I think that's the long and the short of it, I didn't think.' He paused, stirred what was left of his tea. 'So, how do we do this?' he asked.

'I suppose I'd better caution you,' Andy said.

'Then you better had. I don't want you getting into trouble for not doing things properly.'

Andy took a deep breath. 'Ted Eebry, I am arresting you on suspicion of murder. You don't have to say anything . . .'

Ted Eebry watched him closely, pain in his eyes, but something more. He wants my anger, Andy thought. Like he reckoned Kath did. He wants me to punish him.

Caution over, Andy took out his mobile phone and did what he should have done an hour before. He called his boss.

EPILOGUE

It was all a bit of a mess, Rina thought. She felt terribly sorry for Ted and his family, and terribly sorry also for young Andy.

'My fault,' Mac said. 'I left too much for him to do. He wasn't ready for something like this.' He paused at his favourite point of the promenade and looked out to sea.

'Oh, he'll survive,' Rina said. 'It will hurt for a good while, but he'll come out of it wiser and stronger.'

'Will he?'

'I believe so. What happened to Haines? He'll be charged?'

Mac nodded. 'He has powerful legal representation, but the evidence is mounting. It will take time, but when Haines comes to trial it will be a major event.'

'And Vaschinsky?'

'Ah, now Mr Vaschinsky didn't make himself available. He's long gone.'

Rina was thoughtful. 'Do you think there's a chance for Jerry and his wife?'

'I doubt it,' Mac said. 'But I suppose stranger things have happened. Have you talked to George yet?'

'I have, yes. He says he doesn't want anything to do with it, but he'll come round. He's just upset and confused.'

'Maybe it would be best if—'

'If he turned down Karen's gift to him? Mac, he's going to have a hard enough time in the world as it is without imposing further penalties. If he wants to give the whole damned lot away to the local dog's home, well that will be his choice, but I'm not going to deny him options. That wouldn't be right.'

'Do you think she's really gone this time?'

'Karen? Oh, I think so. For the time being, at least. She's completed her mission as Stan calls it. Two bad men dead, others about to be punished and her little brother looked after. Not a bad mission, I wouldn't have thought.'

'It's still murder, Rina. She is still the cause of their death. Others too.'

'And Ted Eebry was the cause of Kath's.'

'The difference being, Ted has spent the rest of his life grieving over it. I doubt Karen will even spare a thought now she's done. I had to tell Kendall what she said to Stan, about Brig Morten. If she ever comes back she'll be arrested, you know that. She's wanted by too many.'

'You took your time telling him,' Rina observed. 'Is there some part of you that hopes she'll stay hidden? That she won't ever be arrested?'

Mac shook his head. 'Rina, I just don't want to have to be the one, you know? Frankly, I don't give much for my chances either, if I crossed Karen again.'

Rina admitted to herself that he was probably right. But despite everything, even despite the fact that Karen was capable of scaring her witless, Rina cherished a certain affection for the girl. She knew it was wrong, but she just couldn't help herself. Karen was alive and intense and it was scarily attractive.

So long, as Mac said, she kept her distance.

'We should go back,' Rina said. 'It's tea time and the boys have been baking. Miriam will be there ahead of us.'

'You didn't tell me what the celebration was?'

'Ah.' Rina smiled. 'My agent called yesterday. The new series has got the go-ahead. We start shooting next spring.'

Mac stopped, took her arm. 'Rina, I'm so pleased for you. But what will that mean? Are you leaving Frantham?'

She shook her head and patted the hand that lay tight about her elbow. 'Oh, no. Frantham is home now, always will be I suspect. I have far too many dear friends here. I'll go and stay wherever we're filming and then come back in between. There's even talk of them looking around here for locations. Lydia Marchant was always more rural sleuth than big city crime fighter, so . . .'

Mac laughed and they turned and walked back along the familiar promenade. 'It will do you good to get a proper job again,' he said. 'Instead of all this amateur sleuthing.'

Rina punched him playfully on the arm. 'I have never ever been an amateur at anything,' she said.

Her arm through Mac's, Rina basked in the contentment of the moment and the exciting times to come, and silently wished Karen well, wherever she might be.

THE END

ALSO BY JANE ADAMS

RINA MARTIN MYSTERY SERIES
Book 1: MURDER ON SEA
Book 2: MURDER ON THE CLIFF
Book 3: MURDER ON THE BOAT
Book 4: MURDER ON THE BEACH
Book 5: MURDER AT THE COUNTRY HOUSE
Book 6: MURDER AT THE PUB

MERROW & CLARKE
Book 1: SAFE

DETECTIVE MIKE CROFT SERIES
Book 1: THE GREENWAY
Book 2: THE SECRETS
Book 3: THEIR FINAL MOMENTS
Book 4: THE LIAR

DETECTIVE RAY FLOWERS SERIES
Book 1: THE APOTHECARY'S DAUGHTER
Book 2: THE UNWILLING SON
Book 3: THE DROWNING MEN
Book 4: THE SISTER'S TWIN

DETECTIVE ROZLYN PRIEST SERIES
Book 1: BURY ME DEEP

STANDALONE
THE OTHER WOMAN
THE WOMAN IN THE PAINTING
THEN SHE WAS DEAD

Thank you for reading this book.

If you enjoyed it please leave feedback on Amazon or Goodreads, and if there is anything we missed or you have a question about, then please get in touch. We appreciate you choosing our book.

Founded in 2014 in Shoreditch, London, we at Joffe Books pride ourselves on our history of innovative publishing. We were thrilled to be shortlisted for Independent Publisher of the Year at the British Book Awards.

www.joffebooks.com

We're very grateful to eagle-eyed readers who take the time to contact us. Please send any errors you find to corrections@joffebooks.com. We'll get them fixed ASAP.

Made in United States
North Haven, CT
29 September 2022

24725593R00139